"I'm here to make a point."

Sawyer leaned closer as he spoke. "We stumbled on to an attraction Friday night that isn't going to go away."

"Please," Faith said, breathing shallowly. "I don't want this, Sawyer. This isn't *you*—"

His mouth took hers. There was none of the teasing, none of the gentleness he'd shown her on Friday night, only the hunger that had been building since then.

Faith attempted to push him away, but he drew her right out of the chair and against him. Immobilized, she tried to keep her mouth closed and rigid, but his lips kneaded the resistance from hers, then rewarded her with a kiss that was wet, warm and unbelievably erotic. She was shaking inside by the time he raised his head.

"Well?" Sawyer demanded, his voice hoarse.

It was a minute before she could say anything. Then she whispered, "You've made your point."

Also available from MIRA Books and
BARBARA DELINSKY

T.L.C.
FULFILLMENT
THROUGH MY EYES
CARDINAL RULES
MONTANA MAN
THE DREAM
THE DREAM UNFOLDS
THE DREAM COMES TRUE

Coming soon

THE OUTSIDER

BARBARA DELINSKY

HAVING FAITH

MIRA BOOKS

MIRA

ISBN 1-55166-271-X

HAVING FAITH

Copyright © 1990 by Barbara Delinsky.

Printed in U.S.A.

HAVING FAITH

1

"**J**ust wait." Laura Leindecker's voice was soft and riddled with pain. "You'll see. He comes across as being honest and charming, and that's what people think he is. That's what I thought he was. For twenty-four years, that's what I thought." She swallowed hard in a bid for strength. "But I know better now. He's not what he seems. He cheats and he lies."

Ignoring the headache that was part and parcel of late afternoon on a hell of a day, Faith Barry came forward, bracing her elbows on her desk. "Did he come right out and confess to having an affair?"

Laura swallowed again. "He had no choice. I found the note. It was right there in the pocket of his trenchcoat. I'm sure he meant for me to find it. He was the one who asked me to take the coat to the dry cleaner, and he knew I'd check the pockets."

"How did he know that?"

"Because I always do it. Bruce is a tight-wad, still he leaves money in his pockets." She frowned. "I think he does it to test me. He's always telling me that I don't really work. But what does he expect," she asked, growing beseechful, "when he has me doing this, that and the other for him all day long? It takes time to see to his custodial needs. But that's my job. So I check his pockets." She paused. "Only there wasn't any money this time." Her voice shook. "Just the note."

Faith nodded, which, aside from injecting an occasional question, was pretty much what she'd been doing for the past fifteen minutes. Laura Leindecker's story wasn't a new one. Faith heard similar ones often, and though the details might differ, the anger, the hurt, the sense of betrayal were the same.

Faith hurt for her. She knew that her questioning didn't help. Still, it was a necessary means to an end. "Can you tell me what the note said?" she asked gently.

Laura looked at the carpeted floor while she gathered her wits. Keeping her lids lowered against humiliation, she said, "'Better than ever. Next week, same time, same place.'" Her eyes rose, filled with hurt. "It was written on notepaper from the Four Seasons. That's our favorite hotel. We've eaten at the restaurant there a dozen times in as many months, and I'm not exaggerating. And he had the gall to take her there."

"To the restaurant?" Faith asked. "Do you think he'd risk that kind of exposure?" She knew of Bruce Leindecker. Most Bostonians did. He'd made his name in real estate, and while he was far from a mega-mogul, his face was well-known.

"I wouldn't put *anything* past him," Laura cried in a moment's lapse of composure. "No decent human being would risk that kind of exposure, but then no decent human being would cheat on a woman who's been faithful and loving and giving and patient and understanding and solicitous for twenty-four years!''

Faith had to marvel at Laura if, indeed, she'd been all those things for so long. Faith had been married for eight years, and in that time she'd only managed to stay faithful. Somehow, all the rest had gone down the tubes—but mutually so. The divorce had been amicable.

"Do you have children?" she asked. She thought she remembered reading about some, but she wasn't sure.

"Two," Laura told her and let out a defeated breath. "They trusted him, too, though it's a miracle. I can't begin to count the number of times over the years when he was to be at a football game or a dance recital and then didn't arrive until the janitors were closing up." She paled when a new thought hit. "I wonder how many of those times he was with a paramour. There were so many opportunities. So many late nights. So many business trips."

"Did you ever suspect anything?"

"No. I told you. I trusted him. I was a fool." She pressed a finger over her lip. When that was ineffective in stanching her tears, she took a handkerchief from her purse, pressed it to her nose, then dabbed at the corners of her eyes.

Faith remembered the first time she'd had a client break down in her office. She'd wanted to put her arms around the woman and tell her everything was going to be all right, except it wasn't true. That particular woman was on welfare, had two preschoolers and chronic asthma, and didn't know how to balance a checkbook, let alone fill out a job application.

Laura Leindecker's situation was different. She was older, for one thing, early fifties, perhaps, and the children were probably grown. She was also more formal, very pretty, elegant in an understated way. She seemed in good health, but Faith knew looks could be deceiving. One thing was sure, though. She wasn't on welfare.

Still, she was in pain. Rich or poor, it didn't matter. Infidelity hurt. Betrayal hurt. The pending dissolution of something that had stood for nearly a quarter century hurt.

Faith waited until Laura was in control again. Quietly she said, ''I know that this is all very difficult for you, Mrs. Leindecker, but if I'm to represent you, I'll have to know more. When you confronted your husband with the note, when he admitted to having the affair, how did he react?''

Laura brooded on that for a minute. ''He was charming.''

''Charming...how?''

''He acted totally humbled. He apologized. He said he'd made a mistake. He almost cried.'' She shot a teary glance skyward. ''Bruce has never cried in his life. Calm, even-tempered, in control—that's Bruce.''

''Perhaps if he nearly cried, it's a sign he was truly sorry.''

''No. It was an act.''

"Maybe he's only now realizing the ramifications of what he's done."

"No doubt," Laura agreed a bit facetiously. "He's wondering where he's going to sleep tonight. I told him I'd call the police if he tried coming home."

Faith was uneasy with threats, particularly ones that would be impossible to enforce. Unless Laura could show that her husband posed a physical danger to her, the police wouldn't do a thing—except report the call in the local newspaper the next week. Once a domestic quarrel went public like that, things were harder to resolve.

"Where were you when you told him this?"

"In his office. When I found that note, I dropped everything and raced right in there. I've never been so angry in my entire life."

Faith could believe that, since Laura struck her as being a relatively sedate soul. But humiliation and hurt often found an outlet in anger.

"He kept telling me to quiet down," Laura went on. "He didn't want anyone in the office to think something was wrong." Her gentle voice went higher. "This is a man who has a weekly tryst with a woman who isn't his wife at a hotel where any number of people can recognize him, and he's worried about being embarrassed at work?" And higher. "Well, what about me? Do you think I'll be able to show my face ever again in that hotel and not be mortified?"

"You will," Faith assured her in a calming tone. "Given who and what your husband is, he was probably discreet."

"At the Four Seasons?"

"There are ways. A room can be taken by the woman. The man arrives after her. No one has to know what floor he goes to or what business he's on. It's simple."

"It's disgusting."

"Yes, but it's done all the time, and with no one the wiser save a wife who finds a note in her husband's coat. Do you have any idea who the woman is?"

"He refused to tell me."

"Do you know how long it's been going on?"

"He wouldn't tell me that, either. He's protecting her. He's afraid I'll go after her in a divorce suit."

"You don't need to go after anyone. Not in this state. The fight won't be about the divorce, just the settlement."

"And I want a big one," Laura said in a show of bravado. "I sacrificed the best years of my life for that man. He was a nobody when I met him. I stood by him through the early years. I was patient. I gave him support. I saw that his needs were filled—" She stopped, looking stricken. Then she grew defensive. "Yes, I *did* fill his needs. It's not my fault that he had to further prove his virility. He should have known better. This is going to cost him."

"It's going to cost you, too, Mrs. Leindecker," Faith felt compelled to point out, albeit gently, "and I'm not only talking about my fee. I'm talking about the emotional pain involved in divorce. You may feel that nothing can be worse than finding a note in your husband's coat pocket, but that's not so. If you decide to file for divorce, things could be harder than you imagine. You'll be alone for the first time in twenty-four years. Have you thought about that? Is it what you want?'' She let the question sink in for a minute. ''And beyond the emotional, there's the physical settlement. If your husband agrees to your demands, that's fine. If he doesn't, the trouble's just begun.''

Laura eyed her warily. ''You're trying to talk me out of this. Why?''

''Because that's my job.''

''I thought your job was to represent me. You have the reputation of being a tough lawyer who fights hard for her clients. I'm willing to pay you to fight hard for me. Why won't you?''

''I will, if that's what you truly want. But as a lawyer, I have a moral obligation to try to salvage the marriage before we end it.'' She couldn't stress the point enough. ''As an officer of the court in this state, I have an *ethical* obligation to do that. No-fault divorce doesn't mean that the marital gates should swing open and shut with the flick of a finger.'' She paused. ''Some people come to me after years of marital counseling and months of discussing divorce. You and your husband haven't done either of those things—at least, not to my knowledge. Have you ever had marital counseling?''

''No.''

''Have you ever considered divorce before?''

''No. I told you. I trusted him. I was completely taken in.''

Faith looked down at her hands, laced and unlaced them, then sat back in her seat. "You had a shock this morning when you found that note. Sometimes a shock like that starts certain wheels moving. They pick up speed and propel you towards something that, if you were to stop and really think about it, you might not want."

Laura clutched the lip of her purse. "I want a divorce."

"You haven't even slept on the thought."

"I want a divorce."

"Are you sure that there isn't the slightest chance of a reconciliation?"

"Yes, I'm sure. I can't trust Bruce anymore. I want a divorce. Will you represent me?"

Faith recognized stubbornness when she saw it, but she had a stubborn streak of her own. "I'll represent you, but only if you go home and think really hard about what you want to do. Today's Friday. If by next Tuesday you still feel that there's no hope for the marriage, I'll help you get your divorce." When she saw Laura pull a checkbook from her purse, she held up a hand. "Wait until Tuesday. If the divorce is what you want, I'll take a retainer then."

"I thought you'd want the money now," Laura said in surprise. "Aren't you afraid that after taking up your time today, I may turn around and go to another lawyer?"

Faith smiled. It was a tired smile, subdued by her headache, not in the least bit smug. But it held pride. "You may, and that's your choice. I think, though, that I offer something unique. I'm a woman and I'm tough. I also happen to get along with most every judge I've faced, and that's what's different here. I'm not strident, like some of my colleagues. I'm not militant. I'm a professional, and a professional gets results. So if results are what you want, you'll be back.''

Laura Leindecker left shortly after that, which was none too soon for Faith who immediately went off in search of a painkiller. Her secretary didn't have any, but she'd half expected that, since Loni was as close to a flower child as a 1990's woman could be. She was sweet and extremely capable, and Faith found a nostalgic charm in her dedication to all things natural and pure, but she had no painkillers.

Nor did Monica, the colleague with whom Faith shared the suite of offices and Loni.

So Faith returned to her desk, determined to beat the headache with sheer willpower, and set about answering the phone calls she'd deliberately left for the end of the day. Several of them were difficult and required adjunctive calls, such as the one to the client suing for custody of her eleven-year-old son, whom she'd just learned was picked up for shoplifting in the local five-and-dime, or the one to the client who had shown up in a hospital the night before with injuries from a beating given her by the husband who, by order of the court, had been forbidden to approach her.

Sheer willpower didn't have much of a chance

against emotional situations like those, and by the time Faith hung up the phone, her headache was no better. So she closed her eyes, put her head in her hands and concentrated on relaxing. But it had been a hard week, and her tension reflected that. She was grateful it was Friday. Though she had plenty of work to do over the weekend, the pace of weekend work was different.

Buoyed by that thought, she reached for a small recorder to dictate several letters. Loni had left for the day, which was fine for the letters since they didn't have to be typed until Monday. It wasn't so fine for the phone. Before Faith had a chance to turn the line over to the answering service, she received back-to-back calls that were both tedious and time-consuming. By the time she finally hung up the phone, she'd just about had it.

That was when the buzzer rang in the outer office. Someone was at the front door of the suite, locked now that Loni was gone. For a minute, Faith considered ignoring it. She considered curling up in a ball in the corner of the sofa, burying her aching head under her arms and shirking every legal responsibility she had. Last time the buzzer had rung after hours, though, it had been a seventeen-year-old girl who had seen Faith on television and wanted help in stopping her parents from making her abort the baby she carried.

Rubbing her temple, Faith left her office. She was barely into the reception area when she felt a wave of warmth. The face beyond the glass door was a familiar one, not a client, but a friend.

She opened the door and smiled up at the tall, dark-haired man who stood there. "Sawyer," she said, almost in a sigh. She slipped her arms around his waist and gave him a hug. "How are you?"

"Better now, sexy lady," he drawled, squeezing her tightly. Then he held her back. "Am I interrupting anything?"

"Work. Always work."

"You work too hard."

"Look who's talking," she scolded, but she was delighted he was there. Taking his hand, she drew him into the office. "I haven't seen you in months. How can that be, Sawyer? We work in the same profession. We work in the same specialty. We even work in the same building. Why don't we ever bump into each other?"

"Good question," he decided. "I think you're avoiding me."

"Me? But you're my best friend!" When he arched a brow, she amended that to, "My best boy friend." When his mouth quirked, she said, "Male friend. My best male friend. I wouldn't have made it through law school without you. Or made it through those early days at Matsker and Lynn. Or had the courage to leave there and go out on my own."

"The feeling's mutual, Faith. You know that." He gave her a quick once-over in appreciation of the fact that she looked professional but individual. Both qualities applied to her practice as well. "I'm proud of you," he said with a grin. "I'm really proud of you. You've done well for yourself."

As she held his gaze, her own grew melancholy. "I suppose."

"What do you mean, you suppose? Look at your practice."

"That's what I've been doing. All week long."

"And you have a headache," he said, suddenly seeing it in her eyes as he'd done countless other times when she'd been under strain. "And," he went on, "you don't have anything to take for it. Why don't you ever buy aspirin?"

"I do. It's at home."

"But you don't need it there. You need it here." Taking her shoulder, he ushered her to the sofa and pushed her down. "Stay put. I'll be right back." Before she could protest, he was out the door and jogging down the hall to the stairs.

She had to smile. Sawyer wasn't an elevator person any more than she was, which was, in fact, how they had originally met. Uptight but eager first-year students, they had literally bumped into each in a stairwell at the law library. Once they'd picked up the scattered books, papers and themselves, they'd started to talk. Though Faith had been black-and-blue for a week from the encounter, the friend she'd found in Sawyer had been worth the discoloration.

She took elevators more now, particularly after hours or when she faced a climb of four or more flights in high heels. Sawyer's office was six floors up. But he was a man, a tall, broad-shouldered man who wasn't worried about rape. Nor was he wearing high heels.

Chuckling at that thought, she put her head back, closed her eyes and sat quietly. In a matter of minutes, Sawyer was back with the pills in his hand. He took a cup of water from the bubbler and waited while she swallowed the aspirin. Then he leaned against Loni's desk with his long legs crossed at the ankles.

"It really *is* pretty amazing," he remarked.

"What is?"

"That we don't run into each other more. I miss seeing you. How've you been?"

She nodded and smiled. "Not bad. Busy. That's good, I guess."

"It is good. How are things at home?"

"Quiet," she said in a voice that was just that. "Lonely sometimes, but it's better this way. More honest. Jack and I went in different directions. For too long we pretended something was left, but it wasn't." She rested her head against the sofa back, but her eyes were fixed intently on Sawyer. "You know what I mean, don't you."

Sawyer knew. And he knew Faith knew he knew, because she'd known his wife. Joanna had needed something else, too. They were married soon after he returned from Vietnam, and for two years she nursed him back to health physically and emotionally. She was good at her job. He had recovered, gone through law school and entered a profession in which he thrived. Joanna hadn't known what to do with the strong and independent man he became. In the end, she found someone who needed her more.

"She married him," he told Faith.

"The fellow with MS?"

He nodded. "She'll devote her life to him. I admire her for that."

"Do you talk with her often?"

"Nah. She's busy. I'm busy. She knows she can come to me if she ever runs into trouble. I owe her a lot. I think I'll always feel that way. But we weren't very good at being husband and wife, and after a while, the constant trying was a strain."

Faith thought about the irony of two divorce lawyers being divorced. "Makes you wonder, doesn't it? Did we go into this field because we knew firsthand the pitfalls of marriage? Or did we see the pitfalls of marriage *because* we went into this field?"

"Had to be the first," Sawyer decided without pause. "We were both having doubts about our marriages even back when we were in law school."

"Not really doubts. Frustrations, and they weren't all that bad. It's just that we talked about them, you and I. Some people don't. Some people suffer year after year in silence. Just this afternoon I met with a woman who wants to end a twenty-four-year marriage. She was telling me that—"

He held up a hand. "Shhh. Don't say it."

"There's not much to say, just that she never thought to—"

"Careful, Faith. That woman is one of the reasons I'm here."

Faith frowned. "Laura Leindecker?"

"Bruce Leindecker. I'm representing him in the divorce."

"You're representing Bruce Leindecker?" Faith repeated. Slowly she sat up. As understanding dawned, she broke into a cautious smile. "You and I—" her finger went back and forth "—are going to be working together?"

"Yup."

She dropped her hand to her lap, and her smile widened. "After all this time. I don't believe it." In the next instant, the smile vanished. "Can we do it? Don't we know each other too well?" But she answered herself in the next breath. "No. There are no grounds for conflict of interest as long as neither of us compromises his client by saying too much. Right?"

"Right," Sawyer said. He folded his arms across his chest.

"Good thing you stopped me a minute ago."

"Uh-huh."

But she was confused. "Who told you I was defending Mrs. Leindecker?"

"Mr. Leindecker."

"How did he know? It's been barely two hours since the woman walked out of here, and we don't even have a formal agreement."

"She seems to think you do. The minute she left you, she called her husband to gloat."

Faith squirmed a little inside. "Gloat—was that his term or yours?"

"Does it matter?"

"Yes. Because it's wrong. Laura Leindecker was angry and hurt. Even if she was the type—which I don't think she is—I doubt she was up for gloating."

"You underestimate the woman," Sawyer said like a man.

"Have you ever met her?"

"No, but her husband knows her well. It sounds like gloating is among the mildest of her faults."

"Sawyer, that man cheated on her," Faith argued, immediately taking the side of her client, which was the rule of thumb in discussions between lawyers. "She's been a loyal wife for twenty-four years and—"

"She has a martyr complex. She's prim and proper and not very flexible when it comes to her husband's business demands. Don't let her con you into believing that she's an angel, Faith. No man turns his back on an angel."

Faith's jaw dropped. "I don't believe this. Are you saying that he was *justified* in philandering?"

"No. All I'm saying is that there are two sides to every story."

"Precisely. That's why we'll take this case before a judge and, if need be, a jury."

"Or settle out of court."

"Or not handle it at all." Her voice mellowed. "Look what just happened. We have to be careful, Sawyer. When we're together we talk. It would be all too easy to discuss things we shouldn't." She chewed on her cheek for a minute, then rose from the sofa and walked to the far side of the room. "This isn't the way I imagined it. I always wanted to work on the *same* side as you. I thought maybe we'd represent codefendants in some kind of civil suit." Turning, she started back toward him. "I don't want to fight you."

He arched a brow. "You can always tell Mrs. Leindecker that you won't represent her."

"But she has a right to representation."

"Let someone else do it."

She stopped talking. "You'd like that, wouldn't you? And your client would like it. He's scared. That was why he called you so quickly. He's scared, because he knows I fight hard." She rather liked that thought. She didn't like the next, though. "Is that why you stopped in here, Sawyer? Did you come to try to talk me off this case?"

"Absolutely not," Sawyer said, coming to his feet. "I want to work with you, even if we are on opposite sides of the case. I've heard you're good. I want to see how good. But if working against me will inhibit you—"

"Why should it?"

"Because we're friends."

"Will our friendship inhibit *you*?"

"Of course not," he said crossly. "A client is a client. Every one deserves the best I can give."

"Should I be different? More partial? More emotional? Should I be making any less of a commitment to my clients than you make to yours?"

"Take it easy, Faith. You're making something out of nothing."

"No," she said, but more thoughtfully. "I know you, Sawyer. Remember the hours we used to spend talking? Remember the times we discussed sexual stereotypes? Remember the times you confessed that you believed women were too emotional for certain types of jobs?"

"I was talking about the presidency of the country, and I still feel that way."

"And I still think you're wrong."

"Fine. Good. I respect that."

She came closer. "I also think your opinions go beyond the presidency. You think women are too emotional, period."

"Not true. Just too emotional for certain jobs."

"Like the presidency."

"I've already said that."

"Or Chairman of the Board of General Motors?"

"What woman is interested in cars? Chairman of the Board of General Foods, now there's a possibility...."

"Sawyer, that's awful!" she cried. She was standing directly before him, hands on hips, chin set. "Talk about stereotypes. You don't have to be interested in cars to be involved with General Motors. You have to be interested in big business and in profits, and if you try to tell me that women aren't economically savvy, I'll scream."

He did his best not to grin. "Calm down, Faith. You're getting too emotional."

"Too emotional?" she echoed, but she saw the humor of the situation. And she couldn't be angry at

Sawyer. He was too nice a guy. "Why is it that when a man raises his voice he's being emphatic, but when a woman does it she's being emotional? Answer me that, Sawyer Bell."

"It's all in the voice. A man's voice—raised—is forceful. A woman's is shrill."

"Is that how you see it in the courtroom?"

"Sometimes."

"And it turns off the judge?"

"Or the jury, or both."

"But we lady lawyers are winning cases. How do you explain that?"

His eyes twinkled. "You lady lawyers who are winning cases have learned to be less emotional and more emphatic."

"That's a compliment, I take it?"

"Definitely."

"Do you see those few female execs of Fortune 500 companies as being more emphatic and less emotional?"

"No doubt."

"But they couldn't be President of the U.S. of A."

"Not yet. They may have come a long way, but they still have a long way to go."

"And women like Margaret Thatcher, Indira Gandhi and Golda Meir?"

He grinned. "They weren't trying to rule countries dominated by male chauvinist pigs."

Faith laughed. She'd forgotten how much fun talking with Sawyer was. As parochial as his views of women were, he knew it, even ridiculed it. In that sense he was probably one of the most liberal men she'd ever met.

Slipping an arm around her shoulder, he drew her to his side. "You laugh, Faith. I like that."

"How can I help it? You're irresistible!"

"So are you." His grin gave way to a look of open-eyed hope. "Come with me tonight. There's a tribute for Dewey O'Day at Parker's. It's going to be boring as hell, but I knew the guy. He gave me good coverage when he was with the *Herald*, so I really have to go. Come with me."

She made a face. "Boring as hell, huh? That's not a great selling point."

"Me. You'll be with me. You'll be helping me survive."

"Sawyer, I hate those things."

"So do I, but I have to go." He cupped her shoulders. "If you go too, we'll have fun. It won't last more than an hour or two."

"Or three. I know these things. They drag on forever."

"We'll sneak out before the speeches begin. In the meantime, there'll be food and booze."

"I don't drink."

"Neither do I, so we'll each have one and we won't be bored at all."

"That sounds totally irresponsible."

"So?"

"What about the case?"

"What case?"

"The Leindecker case. Maybe we shouldn't be seen together."

"That's crazy. We're friends. And colleagues. There's no reason why we can't spend time together. We won't be discussing clients, will we?"

"No."

"So? What do you say?"

"Oh, Sawyer." She let out a breath. "I have so much work to do."

"On Friday night?"

"Yes, on Friday night."

"Do it tomorrow."

"I have other stuff to do tomorrow."

"So you'll have a little more. Come on, Faith. Live a little."

She looked dubious. "At a tribute to Dewey O'Day?"

"With *me*. We'll have a good time. I promise."

Faith tried to think back to the last time she'd had a good time. It seemed ages ago. "You promise?"

"I promise."

2

The room was packed. Everyone who was anyone in Boston political circles was there, as well as members of the business and professional communities who had at one point been touched by Dewey O'Day. That was no small number; the man had been the nose of the *Herald* for forty years. Faith suspected as many people were there to butter up his successor as to pay tribute to Dewey himself. Sawyer confirmed it in a low drawl as they meandered through the crowd.

His whisper swelled to a full voice when he extended a hand to an older man who smiled as they approached. "Senator Cooperthorne. How have you been?"

"Fine, Sawyer."

"Do you know Faith Barry? Faith, this is Peter Cooperthorne, State Senator from Winthrop."

Faith offered her hand and a cordial smile. "It's a pleasure, Senator."

"The pleasure is mine. Good taste, Sawyer. She's a fine-looking woman. Is she yours?"

Sawyer shot Faith an amused glance. "Uh, no. She's a friend. Actually, a lawyer. Actually, a very skilled lawyer. I'm surprised you haven't heard of her. She's something of an authority on family law."

But family law wasn't Peter Cooperthorne's thing, as Faith discovered when he quickly launched into a discussion of the city's latest union dispute. Actually it wasn't so much a discussion as a monologue, and a rambling one at that. Sawyer, who did occasionally dabble in labor law, took the first opportunity to excuse himself and guide Faith away.

"Hot air," he side-mouthed to her. "The man doesn't know diddly about labor psychology, but he has an endless supply of hot air."

"He is the consummate politician," she side-mouthed back, then smiled at a familiar face. "Hi, Tommy. How goes it?"

"Great. But I haven't seen you in a while. You don't come visiting anymore."

Faith sent him a dry look, then made the introductions. "Tommy Lonigan, Sawyer Bell. Tommy is with the Probation Department," she explained to Sawyer. "We've had, uh, mutual clients."

Tommy wasn't leaving it at that. "Faith is the best thing to show her face in the Somerville Court House in years."

"I can believe that," Sawyer said. "Nice meeting you." With a light hand at Faith's back, he started her moving again. "Don't know how he'd know about years," he said under his breath. "He looks like he's fresh out of high school."

"UMass. And he's been out for three years." She nodded at another familiar face, but didn't stop. When

Sawyer swept two glasses of wine from a passing tray and handed her one, she took it. They walked on.

"Sawyer!" A dapper-looking man stopped them. Sawyer introduced him as a former client; Faith recognized him as one of the city's major philanthropists. "So you're paying tribute to old Dewey, too?"

"Sure," Sawyer said. "He's been fair to me."

The man leaned closer and lowered his voice. "Wish I could say the same, but he has a chip on his shoulder when it comes to money. He knocks me in his column every chance he gets, and if it isn't me, it's my car or my house or my art collection. As far as I'm concerned, he should have retired twenty years ago."

"If you feel that way," Faith couldn't help but ask, "why are you here?"

"Because I'm a good sport. And because the governor's showing up later and *he* likes old Dewey." He winked at her, clapped Sawyer on the shoulder and moved on.

Faith looked at Sawyer. "At least he was honest. What do you think he wants from the governor?"

"Probably a job for his new son-in-law. From what I hear, the kid's a real dud." He chinked his wineglass to hers. "Cheers."

"Cheers." She took a swallow and let Sawyer guide her on.

They stopped to greet a mutual acquaintance, a TV reporter who covered the State House and who, when he was off duty, covered himself to the exclusion of most other topics of conversation. Faith thought him a self-centered bore, which she promptly told Sawyer when they finally escaped.

"Not only that," Sawyer announced, "but he sleeps with a teddy bear." He took another swallow of wine.

Faith nearly choked on hers. Laughing, she looked up at him. "A teddy bear? How do you know that?"

"He had an affair with one of the lawyers in our office. She saw the bear."

"Now that's interesting," Faith decided. "Not boring at all." But it was the exception to the rule. For another hour, they wound their way through the crowd, and though they were often stopped by fellow lawyers and other acquaintances, they were never tempted to linger in any one circle for long.

Then the speeches began. "Let's leave," Faith whispered. She and Sawyer were at the back of the room, shoulder to shoulder against the wall. They'd had two glasses of wine apiece, and while they weren't quite tipsy, they weren't quite not. "I'm hungry."

"How can you be hungry?" he whispered back. "You ate a full plate of hors d'oeuvres."

"They were puny and, besides, you ate half of them."

"I did?"

"You did. What would you say to some Peking ravioli and a little Kung Pao shrimp?"

"I'd say, 'Ah so.'"

Faith snickered.

He leaned closer. "Shhh. You'll disturb the MC."

"The MC," she whispered back, "is a lousy speaker. His voice doesn't carry. I can't hear a word he's saying. Who told him to be MC anyway?"

"He's the Speaker of the House. He can do what he wants."

"Except speak."

Sawyer snickered.

"Shhh. You'll disturb the MC."

"You want to listen? I thought you wanted to leave."

"Can we?" she asked, eyes lighting up.

"Not yet. I want to hear Dewey."

"But he'll be last. I know how these things work. A million of his cronies will stand up—"

"Not a million. Maybe a dozen."

"At least a dozen, and they'll tell all kinds of lies—"

"Not lies. They'll talk about his good points and joke about his bad points." He paused. "Yeah, they'll lie." He paused again. "Want to go?"

She grinned. "I thought you'd never ask."

Without another word, they worked their way to the door, crossed through the lobby and went out into the night. A cold blast of air might have cleared their heads some, but the weather was mild, as New England autumns could unexpectedly be. So, lightheaded and lighthearted they headed down School Street.

"Not Chinese," Sawyer said, as though he'd been debating the merits of Kung Pao shrimp ever since Faith had mentioned it. "Want to go to Houlihan's?"

"On a Friday night? We'd never get in."

"Sure we would. All it takes is a ten slipped into the right hand."

But Faith didn't want to go to Houlihan's. "I've been there for lunch three times in the last two weeks. How about Seaside?"

"Talk about lines getting in."

"Talk about slipping a ten—won't it work there?"

But Sawyer didn't want to go to Seaside. "I represented the wife of the owner in a scruffy divorce. Her husband's a bastard. On principle I avoid the place."

Faith could understand that. "How about Zachary's?"

"Too far away. I want to walk. How about the Ritz?"

She screwed up her nose. "Too stuffy."

"And Zachary's isn't?"

"How about the Daily Catch? I want to go to the North End. I feel like squid." She caught his eye. "Do you like squid?"

"I have been known," he said, "to be so mesmerized by the taste of the body of the thing that I forget and leave the tentacles dangling down my chin."

Faith sputtered into a laugh. She looped her arm through his. "You're fun to be with. Jack would never say anything like that. He'd never *do* anything like that."

"So why did you marry him instead of me?"

"Because I didn't know you when I married Jack.

Besides, by the time I met you, you were married to Joanna.''

Sawyer grunted. "She never laughed. She smiled sometimes, but she never laughed. She wasn't the type.'' They turned onto Washington Street and he declared, "Squid sounds just fine. I'm in the mood for the North End. Think there's a festival going on?''

"If there is, we may not get into the Daily Catch.''

"We'll get in.''

"You're slipping tens again?''

"Don't have to. I represented the owner when the city was giving him liquor license trouble. We won. He loves me.''

Faith tried to decide whether she'd heard about that case, but her mind wasn't as sharp as usual. What she did decide was that it didn't matter whether she'd heard about the case or not. "Why is it you have all these illustrious clients? Mine are nowhere near as exciting.''

"So why are you on television all the time?''

"Because I'm attractive, articulate and female.'' She tugged at his arm and drew him down Water Street. "I want to go home and change first. I'll stick out like a sore thumb walking through the North End in a silk dress and heels, and my feet hurt.''

Sawyer was feeling thoroughly agreeable. He had no problem with changing clothes first. And she did have a point. The North End was best enjoyed wearing sneakers. "I'm at Rowes Wharf. You're at Union Wharf. If we stop at my place first, yours is right there on the way to the North End.''

So it was decided. They talked as they walked, laughing most of the way once Sawyer got started on jokes. He had a knack for telling a story, could put on an Irish brogue, an Arkansas drawl or a Brooklyn bark with equal skill, and his repertoire was endless. Some of the jokes were funnier than others, some dirtier than others. Faith was muzzy enough to laugh at anything.

By the time they reached his condo, they were feeling quite good, which was why Faith didn't refuse him when he uncorked a chardonnay and poured her a glass.

"I don't drink," she reminded him as she took a sip of the wine. "Mmm. This is nice."

"It should be. It was a gift from a friend's wine cellar on the occasion of my settling a malpractice suit for him." He sampled the wine, then arched an approving brow. "Not bad."

"Not bad at all. Go change. I'm hungry."

Setting his glass on a coffee table, he headed down the hall. "Make yourself comfortable. I'll be right back."

Faith wandered across the living room. The decor registered in the back of her mind as being modern enough, pleasant enough, coordinated enough. The object of her interest, though, was the view from the window. The harbor's darkness was broken by the lights of passing boats, by buildings flanking the water, by the airport. She could see plenty of boats and buildings from her place, but she had nowhere near as good a view of the airport. Sipping her wine, she watched a plane take off, another one land, a second take off, a second one land.

She loved traveling. She'd done some when she'd been growing up, when her father had still been paying the bills and she'd still had the time. After that, she'd slacked off. Traveling with Jack hadn't been much fun. He wanted to see all the places she'd already seen, busy places like London and Paris, where he could plan out a daily program and sightsee from morning to night. She tried to understand that his job wasn't as demanding as hers. He worked in his father's business, and there was nothing particularly riveting about the manufacture of cardboard boxes. Her job, on the other hand, was both busy and challenging. Her idea of paradise was a long stretch of white sandy beach, a frothy fruit punch and a juicy novel.

So, after a while, she hadn't encouraged Jack to make travel arrangements. She'd contented herself with a week each summer in a rented house on Nantucket, plus whatever legal meetings she could spare the time to attend. But she missed the anticipation of going somewhere new, somewhere just to play.

"Like the view?" Sawyer asked, coming up behind her. He'd changed into jeans and a sweatshirt, and was carrying his wine.

"Oh, yeah." She looked him over. "Not bad, Sawyer. You're staying in shape. Still running?"

"Sure am."

"Every morning?"

"Bright and early. Boston's great at six. Just me and the pigeons and the street cleaners and the dozens of yuppies who live around here and think it's cool to run." He chinked his wineglass to hers. "Cheers."

"Cheers," she said and took a drink. "But you're not a yuppie."

He swallowed his wine. "Nope. Know who is, though?"

"Who?"

He grinned smugly. "Wally Ahearn."

Faith couldn't believe that. "Wally Ahearn? No way. Wally Ahearn was so antiestablishment he was nearly outlawed on the law-school campus."

"But he got his degree."

"Yeah, wearing a gauzy something his guru lent him. Wally Ahearn a yuppie? He *runs*?"

Something about the way she said it—and about the image of Wally as they remembered him in the guru's gown—made them both laugh. Sawyer forced himself to sober, but only after he'd taken a healthy drink of wine. "Trust me, Faith," he said in a trustworthy voice. "Wally no longer looks like a walrus."

"Okay, chalk walrus, and if he's a yuppie, he can't look like a hippie, but I can't, I *can't* see him wearing three-piece suits." She frowned. "He's not actually practicing law, is he?"

"Nope."

"I didn't think so. I always imagined he'd go off to the hills and raise honey bees, or something. Somehow a law degree didn't fit him." She raised the glass to her lips.

"He's a proctologist."

Faith's wine went down the wrong way. Putting a

hand on her chest, she began to cough. Sawyer slapped her back, stopping only when she'd caught her breath. "Why do you *say* things like that?" she cried.

"Because it's true." When she gave a final cough, he said, "Take a drink. It'll help." She took a drink, then a deep breath, and when she'd finished doing that, he drew her to the sofa. "Sit."

"I can't sit," she said. "I want to go home and change, then get something to eat." But she sat. After a minute, she began to laugh. "A proctologist? That's too much."

Sawyer retrieved the wine bottle from the counter that separated the kitchen from the living room. "Have I ever lied to you?"

"No, Sawyer."

"I'm an honorable man." He refilled her wine glass, refilled his own and sank down into the chair across from her. "The last of the good guys." Leaning forward, he chinked his glass to hers. "Cheers."

"Cheers," she said, and took a drink. As the wine warmed her senses, she thought for a minute. "You and Larry O'Neill. The saviors of our class. Where's Larry now?"

"Springfield, Illinois. He's doing tax work."

"I can believe that. He has a big family to support. How many kids now?"

"Eight."

"No!"

But Sawyer nodded. "So help me, eight kids."

"He had three when we graduated, and that was nine years ago. He's been busy."

Sawyer laughed. "His wife is the busy one. Do you remember her?"

"Charlene? Of course, I remember Charlene. She was always pregnant. Still is, I guess." She raised her glass. "To Charlene."

"To Charlene," Sawyer said and took a drink. "So how about you, Faith? Do you want kids?"

"Sure I do. I want twelve."

"Twelve!"

"Three sets of twins and two sets of triplets."

"I can't picture it."

"Why not?" she asked, sounding hurt. "Doctors can do anything nowadays. I put in my order, they get out their little test tubes and their little petri dishes, I get my kids."

"Ahhh," he said sagely.

"That's right, ahhh. So how about you?"

"Me? No way. I'm not getting pregnant with one, let alone twins and triplets. Don't want to ruin my figure."

She laughed, and a grin remained long after the sound had died. She sat back in the sofa, feeling more relaxed than she had in months and months. "You're fun, Sawyer. How could I have forgotten that?"

"Out of sight, out of mind."

"But we always had such good times. Remember the lunches we had with Alvin Breen? Or the seminars we went to? Remember the time we served on a panel together in Pittsfield?"

"Do I ever," he said. There was a wry twist to his lips and a playful gleam in his eye. "You were the only woman, and you took advantage of it to the hilt. You wore a bright red dress, bright red shoes, bright red lipstick, bright red nail polish, and you sat there looking like a perfect piece of fluff. Boy, did you fool them. Their mouths dropped open when you began to speak."

Faith sipped her wine, then said with an innocent tip of her head, "It wasn't my fault they thought I was dumb."

"You let them believe it, you shameless hussy."

"They *chose* to believe it. Most men do."

"Doesn't it make you mad?"

"Mad? When I get such satisfaction seeing them with egg on their faces?"

Sawyer threw back his head and laughed. "I love it," he said, then sat forward. "You're remarkable." He chinked his wineglass to hers. "To you."

"To me," she said with a grin and, with a flourish, finished her wine. She was feeling delightfully warm. Any rough edges that were left over from the week had melted away.

Sawyer rose, took the wine glass from her and set it on the table, then grabbed her hand and drew her up. "Let's go. I'm hungry."

"I think I'm a little high."

"Me, too. We need food."

Minutes later, they were heading down Atlantic Avenue in the general direction of Faith's place.

"This is fun," he announced. "I haven't done anything spontaneous in a long time."

"Me, neither. My life is predictable. There's work, work and more work."

"Ever get tired of it?"

"Yup. Then the phone rings, I get a new case and I'm revived."

They walked along at a jaunty pace.

"You're not really representing Dorothea Winchell, are you?" Sawyer asked.

"Sure am."

"She's a fraud."

Faith wasn't at all offended. "Uh-uh. She loved the man. She was with him for ten years. Ten years. And in that time, she took a lot of abuse."

"He chose not to leave her anything in his will."

"He had Alzheimer's. Did he choose, or was he unable to choose? Or did his children prevent him from choosing?"

"You'll lose," Sawyer warned, but playfully. That was the kind of mood he was in.

Faith was in a similar mood. "Losing is relative. As his common-law wife, she has a right to a little protection. We won't get all we're asking, but something is better than nothing." She sent a perky look up at him. "And you're a fine one to be talking. You're representing John Donato. Now, if that isn't a lost cause, I don't know what is."

He was undaunted. "It's a *great* cause. Donato puts up a building. Halfway through construction, the city council finds an obscure code that says the building can't be that tall. Donato is expected to lower the building at a million dollar loss. The city owes him.''

"From what I hear,'' Faith drawled, looking off toward the Aquarium, "Donato obtained his original permit in a slightly, uh, unorthodox manner.''

"Y'heard that, did ya?''

"Yup.''

"Who'd you hear it from?''

"I'm not telling. Is it true?''

"Now, if I told you that, it'd be a violation of lawyer-client privilege.''

"I won't tell anyone,'' she whispered loudly.

In answer, he wrapped an arm around her waist and pulled her close. Their hips bumped. Laughing, they adjusted their gaits to match, and walked on. To the left, the lights of the Marketplace lent a gaiety to the night. To the right, the Harbor was unusually serene. They felt peaceful, happy, totally at ease with the night and each other, and because of that, they talked about things they might not have normally discussed.

Such as the people they'd dated since their respective divorces.

"Brandi Payne? You actually went out with Brandi Payne?'' Faith asked in good-humored disbelief as they turned into Union Wharf.

"Sure did.''

"I hear she's a bitch.''

"You hear right. She gives new meaning to the term swelled-headed. I suppose you have to give her some credit. She came in as the Channel 4 anchor when the station was trailing the other two, and she's brought it to the top. But full of herself? Whew!''

"What possessed you to go out with her?"

"We have a mutual friend. He had a party. We met. I asked her out. I wanted to see what the private persona was like, and boy, did I ever. We ran into Alec Soames and Susan Siler at the restaurant. They were in town to do a signing at the Ritz, and they happen to be a stunning couple. Brandi didn't like that much. She wants all eyes on her. The comments she made to Alec and Susan about their book were bad enough, but the fuss she made about what table we were going to have and whether the service was good enough and whether the butternut squash soup had too much salt were downright embarrassing.''

"Poor Alec and Susan."

"Poor Sawyer."

Faith was grinning as she opened the door to her condo. "What I want to know," she said, punching out the code to turn off the alarm, "is whether you took her to bed." When the alarm didn't stop, she frowned, concentrated, punched out the code a second time.

"That's a very personal question."

"You're a very personal friend. Damn, what's wrong with this?" The alarm was still humming, waiting to be disengaged. Slowly and with deliberation this time, she gave separate emphasis to each digit in the code. Still the alarm resisted. "I don't believe it," she cried.

"Are you hitting the right numbers?"

"I'm hitting 4-3-8-3. That's my phone number." She put two fingers to her forehead and closed her eyes. "Alarm code. 8-2-9-2." She had punched in the first two when noise exploded around them. The noise died just as suddenly when she entered the last 2. She grinned up at Sawyer. "There. All better. But you didn't answer my question. Did you sleep with Brandi Payne?"

"No, I did not."

"Why not? She has a great bod."

"By the time we finished dinner, I was so turned off by the woman herself that I didn't give a damn about her bod." The phone rang. "Good timing," he said and started toward it. Abruptly he stopped. "Uh, it's yours."

Laughing, Faith turned into the kitchen and answered it. "Yes?" She grew serious. "Emergency 24?" She frowned. "My alarm. Oh, my alarm! I'm so sorry. That was a mistake. I confused my phone number with—no, no, there's no need to call the police. The code? Uh, uh, 3-6-5. Yes. Thank you." She hung up the phone and looked at Sawyer, who was leaning against the doorjamb. "They wanted to make sure I was okay. Wasn't that nice? If I hadn't given them the right code, they'd have called the police. It's a very clever system. As you can see, none of my neighbors have come running to the door to see whether it's me or a burglar in here." She thought for a minute. "Maybe I need a dog. You know, something intimidating. A watchdog."

"But you're afraid of dogs."

"How do you know?"

"I was with you once when you were attacked by a poodle. Don't you remember? It was four or five years ago. We'd just come from lunch at Dini's, and there was this adorable little—"

"Adorable, nothing!" Faith cried, remembering the day. "That dog was vicious! It was coming right at me with its teeth bared."

"You *thought* it was coming right at you, but the fact was that it was headed for a schnauzer behind you. And it didn't have its teeth bared. It was grinning." He chuckled. "Boy, were you scared."

"And you laughed. You laughed at me."

"I couldn't help it. It was funny. You're always so serene-looking, even when you're in court, and then this little dog comes along and—"

"I'm going to change," she interrupted. "I'm hungry."

"Good idea. What's this?"

She had taken a bottle from under a cupboard and was putting it in his hands. "Champagne."

"I think I've had enough to drink."

"So have I. But this is special champagne. It was given to me by Dennis and MaryAnn Johnson when we finally found the right baby for them to adopt. The agencies had given them trouble, because Dennis was convicted of marijuana possession eighteen years ago. Not a spot of trouble since, still he has a record. So we went the private route. It took two years, but the baby is perfect." She grinned. "So this is happy champagne. Open it."

Sawyer looked at the bottle. "Happy champagne, huh?" He was certainly happy. "Why not. You go change, while I open it. I'm feeling underdressed."

Faith leaned close, stretched up to his ear and whispered, "Better underdressed than undressed." She came back down, eyeing him quizzically. "I've never seen you undressed. Do you know that, Sawyer? I've never even seen you without a shirt on. Why didn't we ever go to the beach?"

"We were too busy."

"We went to movies. You and Joanna and Jack and me. Why not to the beach?"

"The beach is for vacations. We never vacationed together."

"Why not? It would have been fun."

"Maybe we didn't trust ourselves. Go change, Faith. I'm hungry."

"Mmm. Me, too," she murmured and went off toward her room.

Sawyer managed to uncork the champagne without too much trouble. He had more trouble finding fluted glasses, then laughed when he realized what he'd gone looking for. Faith wouldn't have fluted glasses any more than he would. A few wine glasses, yes. Wine glasses were good to have on hand in case company popped in with a bottle. Fluted glasses were for more sophisticated drinking, and since Jack hadn't imbibed any more than Joanna, there were no fluted glasses here.

So he took two wine glasses, filled them with champagne and ambled into the living room. It was small and didn't have much furniture, but what it did have was in good taste. Faith had that. Joanna didn't, which wasn't to say that he hadn't liked the house they'd shared. It had been an old thing on the outskirts of Cambridge. They'd bought it soon after they married, thinking that renovating it would be good therapy for Sawyer, and it had been that. He'd taken pride in stripping and staining the woodwork, putting in a new floor, updating the kitchen. It had given him a sense of accomplishment. Joanna's satisfaction came through his—and through filling the place with homespun things. Nothing matched. She had no eye for style or design. She created a cozy clutter that, unfortunately, began to grate on Sawyer when he grew to want breathing space.

Faith's place, small though it was, had breathing space. He was amazed that he thought so, since he'd had enough wine to create the illusion of closeness and warmth, but he felt perfectly comfortable here.

He walked around the sofa and perched against its back, which ran parallel to the glass sliders that looked out on the harbor. Actually, he mused, the view was sideways. It took in as much of the city as the harbor. As for details, he couldn't see many. The glass was reflecting the room behind him more strongly than anything else.

"Cheers," he said, and held one of the wine glasses out toward his reflection in the glass. He was about to take a sip when his reflection was joined by Faith's. She was wearing jeans and a sweatshirt, and without her heels, seemed suddenly more petite.

"Come," he told her reflection. "I want to make a toast."

"Another toast," she breathed. Rounding the sofa, she came to his side and took one of the glasses. "Cheers," she said.

"*I* want to make the toast."

She stopped the glass an inch before her mouth. "Okay. You make the toast."

"Cheers," he said and took a drink.

She laughed, declared his toast, "Profound," and sipped the champagne. "Ah," she said when the last of the bubbles had slipped down her throat. "Nice. Did you miss me?"

"Sure did. I was trying to look out your window, but I couldn't."

"Wait," she said. Holding her glass to the side, she went back through the room and turned off the light. "There." She returned to the nook he'd found behind the sofa. "Like it?"

He stood and moved close to the glass. "Oh, yeah. It's different from mine. You can see the city. And the boats in their slips. You even have a patio."

"You have a balcony."

"This is different. Must be the trees. How did you manage to get trees in here?"

"Sanguinetti Landscaping. They specialize in potted things. Nice flowers and shrubs and plants and stuff. I wanted green."

He turned to look at her. She was faintly lit by the reflection of the city lights, and seemed almost

ephemeral. "You're a very wise girl. I don't understand why some man hasn't snapped you up yet."

"I've only been divorced for a year."

"But you're a catch." He returned to the sofa and
sat close by her side. "Didn't someone tell me you
dated Paul Agnes for a while?"

"Twice. We went out twice."

"Didn't like him?"

She sipped her champagne. "Not enough."

"To go to bed with him?"

"Right. That was pretty much all he wanted. Why
was that, Sawyer? Why *is* that? I thought times had
changed. I thought AIDS had put the fear of God into
singles. But sex has been the one thing that's first and
foremost on the minds of the men I've seen since the
divorce. Not that I've seen that many. I'm not in a
rush to get involved with anyone. I'm busy with
work. I rather like being able to come and go as I
please. And I'm not lonely, except sometimes a guy
will ask me out for dinner or to a show and it sounds
like fun. So I go. And it is fun, until we get back here
and he wants to come in. If I say no, he's angry. If I
say yes, he's into touchy and feely before you can
blink an eye, and when I say no to that, he's doubly
angry. So I'm damned both ways. It shouldn't have
to be like that."

Sawyer, who'd been sampling his champagne, set
the stem of the glass on his knee. "Know what your
problem is?"

"No, what? Tell me. I want to know."

"You're too pretty."

"There's no such thing."

"There is, and you are. You're a striking woman. It may be the way you dress. Or the way you carry yourself. Or your confidence. You're feminine without trying to be. It's hard for a man to look at you and not think of sex."

"You don't."

He took a larger swallow from his glass. "That's 'cause you're Jack's girl. You've always been off-limits to me, so I look at you other ways. I know how intelligent and creative and honest and fun you are to be with."

She sent him a glowing smile. "You are my favorite man." She slipped an arm around his waist and raised the other, glass in hand. "To you," she declared.

"To me," he echoed.

They both drank deeply of the champagne. Sawyer slipped from her side. "Hold still. Don't move." He half-walked, half-ran back to the kitchen, scooped up the champagne bottle and was back.

"Maybe we shouldn't," Faith whispered as she watched him refill their glasses. "I'm hungry."

"Me, too, but we haven't finished with the toasts." Setting the bottle on the floor, he sat beside her again and raised his glass. "To Jack and Joanna."

"Why are we toasting them?"

"Because they're not here to toast themselves."

"But why do they have to be toasted?"

"Because they're good sports. They put up with

us." He chuckled, then pulled a straight face. "To Jack and Joanna." He chinked his glass to hers.

"To Jack and Joanna," Faith said and took a drink. Since there were two people in the toast—and since Sawyer seemed to be doing it—she took a second drink on the heels of the first. "Sawyer?"

"Umm?"

"Maybe we should fix them up."

"Jack and Joanna? Nah. Wouldn't work. Joanna's too maternal."

"Jack's paternal. It would be great."

"Only if they had a kid, but they'd never make it in the sack."

"That's an awful thing to say, Sawyer!"

He considered that for a minute. "Yes. I'm sorry." He looked at Faith.

She looked at him. "You're not sorry at all."

"No."

They laughed. This time it was Sawyer who slipped an arm around Faith's waist. "I can tell you anything. Do you know how nice that is?" He tugged her close to give her a hug, but somehow they lost hold of their perch on the back of the sofa and half-slid, half-fell to the floor. That made them laugh harder.

"Ahhh," Sawyer groaned through his laughter. "Are you okay, Faith?"

"I'm down, but not out," she declared with mock pomposity. More humbly, she said, "Something spattered on my sweatshirt. Am I bleeding?"

"That was champagne. Com'ere." He helped re-arrange her body so they were tucked snugly against the sofa and each other, facing the world beyond the glass sliders. Taking only a minute to replenish their glasses of any champagne they may have lost in the fall, he picked up where he'd left off.

"You're special. I don't know any other woman I can do this with. I really can tell you anything. Anything."

From time to time, one word slurred into the next, but it was subtle, too subtle for Faith, in her own less-than-sober state, to notice. "Tell me something," she said. She tapped his chest with her finger. "Tell me something you wouldn't tell anyone else."

He lowered his voice to a whisper. "Joanna was a lousy kisser."

"A lousy kisser? But she was a nurse. What about all that mouth-to-mouth—"

They burst into hysterics, leaning over one another in laughter. Sawyer was the first to recover. "Honest to God, I don't know how she ever did that. When it came time to kiss, she didn't open her mouth. I couldn't get her to open her mouth."

"And I'm sure you were persuasive."

"I tried. She didn't like the feel of it. So I stopped trying after a while." He looked down at her face in the darkness. "Was Jack persuasive?"

"No. He was punctual."

"Punctual? What's punctual got to do with kissing?"

"Jack was a systematic lover. Certain things were to be done certain ways at certain times, and that was that. Kisses were a meeting of the mouth. They started out as pecks. After seventy-seven seconds of that, they became smooches, and after two minutes and ten seconds of that, they got wet. They stopped completely when he began to pant.''

"Sounds like a dog," Sawyer observed, and they broke up again. This time when they sobered, Faith set her wine glass aside. Levering herself up with a hand on his chest, she faced him.

"Show me," she ordered. "Show me how you kissed her."

Something in the back of Sawyer's hazy mind told him that would be wrong. "I can't. I've forgotten."

"Then show me how you kiss, period. I'll bet you're good. I want to know what a good kiss is like."

"So do I."

She cupped his face with her hands. "Kiss me, Sawyer. Show me how you do it. Please?"

Sawyer looked at her upturned face, so dimly lit as they sat on the floor behind the sofa. He looked out at the city, where thousands and thousands of people were enjoying each other, and he wanted to enjoy himself, too. He *was* enjoying himself.

But he wanted to kiss Faith.

For a long moment he thought, or tried to think of the reasons why he shouldn't. But he was high. He couldn't come up with a single one.

3

"How I kiss," he said softly. He raised both hands and slid them into her hair so that he could frame her head and tip it up. "The first touch isn't much more than a token. It's kind of like a hello."

"Is this what you used to do when you walked in from work?"

"No. That wasn't much more than a peck on the cheek, and sometimes it wasn't even that. I thought you wanted to know what a *kiss* kiss was like."

"I do."

"A sex kiss?" he asked, daring it because the wine had loosened his tongue.

"Mmm."

"Okay. First, there's this." He lowered his head, put his lips on hers and moved them just a little before lifting his head again. "It's a way of me finding out if you want to be kissed. Sometimes Joanna didn't. Sometimes she'd turn her head. No way I could miss that message. You, on the other hand—" he gave a skewed grin "—didn't pull away, so I can guess that you want more."

Faith did. "That little thing was just a teaser."

"That's what it was supposed to be. It's supposed to make you want more."

"The first step in persuasion? Okay. So what do you do next?"

"More of the same." Lowering his head again, he did just that. One light touch after another, each gentle but enchanting, none lasting long enough to provide any deep satisfaction.

Faith liked the way his lips could be firm but still gentle. She liked the warmth of his breath and the faint smell of wine. She liked the feeling of leisure. "Mmm. This is nice. Jack would have already moved on. He had to keep on schedule. But this is nice."

Sawyer agreed. He continued to dole out those fetching kisses, because they were captivating even him. In between, he talked. "Schedules don't work when it comes to sex." He brushed the upper bow of her mouth. "The thing is that sometimes after that first hello you want it hard and fast." He sampled the corner of her mouth. "Other times you want it slow. Sometimes," he said, pausing to kiss her chin, "you want to widen your focus a little. Sometimes a woman's mouth makes you curious about how other parts of her taste." He slid his mouth up to her cheek, then her eye, kissing each lightly. He came down the gentle slope of her nose in an inevitable return to her mouth. "Sometimes," he whispered, "you even want to taste with your tongue." He did that, tracing the curve of her mouth, then sucking in a shallow breath. "Mmm, Faith. You taste very good."

Faith's eyes were closed. She felt as though she

were floating, no doubt, she reasoned, on the champagne bubbles that shimmered inside her. "Jack never told me that," she said. Her words were wispy and seemed to overlap. "He never talked when he touched me. He was letting his body do the speaking, only I could never hear the words. Why was that?"

"Maybe because you were concentrating on what was going to happen next. That's what Joanna always did. She didn't want to linger. Move right along, folks. Come on, keep going. She wanted to get on with it and get done as soon as possible. She wanted to get it over with."

"I didn't want that," Faith protested, then hesitated. "Well, maybe I did. There was nothing inspiring about what was happening. I never enjoyed Jack's kisses. Certainly not the way I'm enjoying yours. Go on, Sawyer. Kiss me more. I liked what you were doing."

So Sawyer kissed her more, still those same first-stage kisses that he was finding so pleasurable. He knew that the wine had put a glowing sheen on his awareness of the world. He also knew that Faith was a friend, not a sex partner, but that didn't stop him from enjoying the scent of her skin and the dewiness of her mouth. Her lips were soft and pliant, just as a woman's should be. She wasn't reticent, as Joanna had been. Nor was she aggressive, as some other women could be. She let him set the pace, and she responded to it. She seemed very much in tune with him. He liked that.

When he caught a soft sigh slipping from her lips,

he opened his mouth to catch it. Her sigh became a gasp, and he quickly pulled back. "You don't like that?"

"I do." She laughed. "I do. It surprised me, that's all. Do it again. I'll be ready this time."

She tried to be, still she wasn't prepared for what happened when Sawyer opened his mouth on hers and gave her the kind of kiss he was primed for. The soft hellos and gently foraging smooches gave way to deeper curiosity. But he didn't have to force her mouth open. It moved with his, reacting to his in all the ways that seemed perfectly natural and utterly right. So he kissed her more deeply, then more deeply again. His tongue found hers, went beyond and around it, swept through the inside of her mouth in a journey that took his breath away.

He gasped for air and tried to steady the fine tremor that shook his arms. "Whew. That's never happened to me before."

"What?" she whispered. She was taking small, short breaths.

"Getting caught up like that."

"You didn't get caught up with Joanna? I always thought men had to get caught up if they were going to be able to complete the sex act."

"Right," he said, "but at different times and levels. Was Jack always ready at the start?"

"Hard, you mean?"

"Hard, I mean."

"Yes. Jack made up his mind that it was time to make love and, bingo, he was hard. I sometimes wondered whether he needed me at all. It could have been anyone under him.''

''That's not true. He loved you.''

''In his way, but that kind of love had little to do with the sex we had. I'm telling you. It was preprogrammed sex. Nothing like what we're doing now.'' Her voice dropped to a whisper. ''What do we do next?''

Sawyer was still too aware of her taste on his tongue. Taking his hands from her hair, he sat against the sofa back. ''Next we take a break.''

''Why?''

''Because I need to catch my breath.'' It was more than that, he knew. It was a tiny voice inside telling him that something was going to get out of hand if he didn't slow down. He was feeling too good. Whether it was the wine or Faith, he didn't know, but his blood was pumping a little too warmly through his veins. And that last, deep, tongue-twisting kiss had done something to his groin. Things were beginning to feel tight down there. He needed a break.

Reaching for his wine glass, he took a swallow.

Faith was sitting up, eyeing him through the darkness. ''You didn't like it,'' she whispered, and even in spite of the non-sound of her voice, he caught bits of accusation and hurt.

He put a hand to her cheek. ''I liked it too well.'' Slipping his hand down, he caught one of hers and flattened it over his heart. ''Feel that? Is that the feel of something I don't like?''

''Could be,'' she said, pouting. She'd never pouted

before in her life. She hated people who pouted and would have hated herself—if she'd known. "People's hearts bang when they're upset or afraid. Could be that you don't want to be doing this, but you feel you have to since I asked. Is that it?"

"No way! If I didn't want to be doing this, I'd get up off the rug and walk away. Do you see me doing that?"

"Maybe you're too tired."

"I'm not too tired."

"Or drunk. Maybe your legs won't work."

He set the wine glass aside. "They work just fine. And I am not drunk," he insisted. He tried to put separate emphasis on each word, but they slurred together. Pulling her across his lap and into his arms, he declared, "I liked what I was doing. I'm going to do it again."

But what he did was different. At least, Faith thought it was. Not that she could remember the fine details of what he'd done before, since the amount of wine she'd drunk robbed her of that clarity, but she remembered the titillation of it. What he did now was even more titillating. It was bolder, more confident, persuasive in ways that had nothing to do with clarity and everything to do with pure sensation. By the time he ended the kiss, she was grasping his sweatshirt for dear life.

"Is *that* how you kissed Joanna?" she whispered between short gasps.

He didn't know. He hadn't been consciously thinking of Joanna. He hadn't been consciously thinking of much but the fire that licked at his nerve ends.

"Maybe we'd better stop," he whispered back. Her head was cradled in his arm. He looked down at her face to find features whose eagerness shone through the dim night light.

"I don't want to stop. I want you to show me more." She bobbed up. With the sudden movement, she swayed. Steadying herself, she sat on her haunches between his legs. "I want to do something."

"What?"

"Touch you. Jack didn't like being touched. He didn't think it was important. He didn't need it to be aroused. But it might have helped me." She averted her eyes in a moment's reconsideration. "Maybe not. Jack had a nice enough build, but there was nothing spectacular about it. Maybe my touching him wouldn't have done a thing for either of us." She looked back up at Sawyer and whispered. "Let me touch you. Just a little." She relaxed her grip on his sweatshirt and flattened her hands on his shoulders. Slowly she drew them toward his neck, back to the top of his arms, almost timidly down over the musculature of his upper chest. And everywhere her hands went, her eyes followed.

She let out a single, clipped sound, halfway between a sigh and a gasp. "Like this," she whispered. "Just like this. So nice."

Sawyer didn't know whether he was more pleased with the look of awe on her face or the feel of her hands on his chest. "Wait." His voice was sounding hoarse. "I'll make it even better." Before either of them could begin to wonder whether they were going too far, he whipped the sweatshirt over his head.

Faith sat back on her heels, looking at what he'd bared. "Sawyer, you're so big!"

"Is that good or bad?"

"Good! Good! I hadn't realized..." Her voice trailed off when she brought her hands up and touched him. His skin was warm, even hot, but she was truly stunned by how much of him there was. She'd known he was well-toned, but she hadn't known he was so broad in the shoulders. Moving in a slow, dreamy way, her hands took forever to cover him. Part of that was because the hair on his chest slowed her down. It created a friction that she found surprisingly exciting. Where the hair thinned and tapered into a narrow line, she purposely kept her hand slow to fully appreciate the firmness of his skin.

Sawyer had never been so erotically charted. He leveled his shoulders, took in a deep gulp of air that expanded his chest even more. With that oxygen feeding his brain, he grabbed Faith under the arms and drew her forward. His mouth met hers in a kiss that, for the first time, held raw hunger.

It should have frightened Faith off, or at least alerted her to the fact of his arousal. But she was too aroused, herself, to think of anything but enjoying more. Wrapping her arms around his neck, she immersed herself in the kiss. Somewhere in its midst, he began to caress her breasts, but that fact was lost amid the overall headiness of what she felt.

"Hold on for a second, babe," he dragged his mouth from hers to whisper. He tried to ease her away but she made a throaty sound of protest and tightened her grip on him. Reaching back for her wrists, he dragged them forward. "Wait. I want to touch you." He held her gaze while he covered her breasts with his hands. After a second he began to knead her flesh. It was the most wonderful thing Faith had felt yet. Her expression told him so.

"Didn't Jack do this to you?"

She nodded. "But it didn't feel like this."

"What does it feel like?"

"Good. I don't know. Really good. Did Joanna like it when you touched her breasts?"

He shook his head. "It embarrassed her. Does it embarrass you?"

Faith swallowed. She was breathing more quickly again, and he wasn't even kissing her anymore. "No. It makes me hot."

"I want to take off your shirt."

"Maybe you·shouldn't. Maybe this is enough." But he chose that minute to rub his thumbs over her nipples, which were distinct even through her bra and sweatshirt. "Mmm, do it." She reached for the hem herself, and while she was pulling the sweatshirt over her head, Sawyer unhooked her bra. By the time she lowered her arms, she was naked from the waist up. For a minute, she sat very still looking up at him. Her expression would have been wary if her features were working right, but they didn't seem to be responding efficiently to the commands of her brain. "Is this right, what we're doing?" she managed to ask. She was feeling warm and tingly and more than a little muzzy.

"Oh, yeah," he professed a bit brashly. "We're the best of friends, Faith. Nothing between us is wrong. Here." He held his wine glass to her lips and gave her a drink, then took one himself. Then he set the glass aside and touched her. "You have very beautiful breasts. They stand there, just waiting for me."

"Joanna's didn't stand there?"

"They sagged."

She sputtered out a laugh. "You're awful!"

"I'm serious," he said, but softly. His eyes didn't stray from her breasts, and as he talked, his hand moved lightly, if a bit unsteadily over her flesh. "I didn't really see them much. She kept them well hidden. I think she was ashamed of her body." Raising his eyes to hers, he said, "You're not. I can feel it in you. You're proud to be a woman. That's really refreshing, Faith. Do you know how refreshing it is?"

For a minute, Faith couldn't say a word. He was brushing his fingers over the tips of her breasts. She fancied there was a wire stretching from that point to another point deep inside her. With each brush of his fingers the wire twisted.

"Faith?"

"Mmm?"

"Are you okay?"

"I think so."

"How does that feel?"

"Incredibly—" Her voice caught. She tried again. "Incredibly nice." But just then, the wire snapped. She came forward and up on her knees, looking for his kiss. He gave it to her with just the force she needed, but even before the kiss was over, the hunger had grown. Hugging him tightly, she cried, "Sawyer?" Her mouth was by his ear, her high-pitched cry urgent.

"What is it, sweetheart?"

"Something's hurting. I'm feeling so empty inside that it's hurting. Help me. Please, help me."

Sawyer was feeling the same hurt. It had managed to surface through the aura of pleasure that was clouding his view of reality. "Shhh, it's okay, sweetheart." He held her tightly for a minute, but the feel of her bare back beneath his arms, not to mention the heaven of her breasts against his chest, drove him on. "Okay," he whispered. He took her mouth in a kiss at the same time that he reached for the snap of her jeans. The zipper was quickly down. She scrambled back to push at the denim and her panties. Together they shimmied both from her legs. Then, while he ran his hands over the parts of her body that were newly uncovered, she hurriedly worked at his jeans.

His zipper was more difficult to lower than hers had been. He was fully aroused, and while that hindered her progress, the discovery excited her beyond belief. No sooner was his fly open when she slipped both hands into his briefs and found the heat waiting there.

"Oh my," she murmured. "Oh my."

"'Oh my' is right," he growled. Tumbling her backward onto the carpet, he quickly shucked his pants. He had to be inside her. There wasn't any doubt in his mind that if he didn't make it fast, he'd die of frustration. Her thighs were open. She rose to meet him when he came between them, and when he entered her, she cried out.

It was the heat. He knew because he felt it himself. It was the heat and the moisture and the wine that made her sheathing so perfect. He tried to savor it, tried to move in and out with the proper understanding of how well she fit him, but he didn't have the patience. He was burning from the inside out, and the only way to fight that was to surge hard and deep toward fulfillment.

Faith was with him all the way. She goaded him on with the movement of her hips, her legs, her restless hands. Their bodies grew damp with sweat, and the sweat mingled. They drove each other ever higher. And when he reached the release he sought, the spasms of his body beat against and between her throbbing.

That should have been the end of it. They should have fallen apart on the floor, done in by drink or exhaustion or sheer bliss. Somehow, it didn't work that way. They did lie there for a minute until they'd caught their breath. But then it was as if they forgot they'd climaxed. Sawyer was still hard inside her, and when he began to move, she gasped in delight.

It took longer this time. Their movements were slower, more drugged, but no less pleasurable. After a time, it was hard to tell where one peak ended and the next began.

Faith came awake very reluctantly the next morning. On the one hand, things were as always. She was in her bed, where she was every morning when the sun rose over the harbor and skipped sideways into her window. On the other hand, things were different.

Her head hurt, for starters. She discovered that when she tried to move it around on the pillow. Her eyes hurt, too. She opened them a slit, immediately realized her mistake and shut them again.

And she was naked. The sheets felt different against bare skin. Moving a hand to her ribs, she confirmed the finding, but that didn't make it any easier to understand. She never slept naked. She was usually too cold for that. Winter or summer, it didn't matter, she always wore something, preferably long-sleeved and ankle length, to bed.

She was warm, though, and for an instant she wondered whether she'd set the electric blanket higher than usual. But she didn't have the electric blanket on. At least she didn't think she did. It was still in storage. And yet she was warm. Gingerly exploring that warmth, she moved her leg. In the process, she discovered two things.

The first was that her muscles hurt. Not just any

old muscles, but those in her legs. To be exact, those in her thighs.

The second was that she wasn't alone. Her foot had hit something solid. It was the source of the heat, she knew. She also knew that it had been well over a year since she'd shared a bed with Jack. She hadn't shared a bed with any other person since.

Momentarily ignoring the pounding in her head and the ache around her eyes, she forced herself to look at the side of the double bed that was usually vacant. It wasn't vacant now. A head capped with dark, rumpled hair was in possession of the second pillow. Just below that head was a sinewed neck, below that a pair of broad shoulders, below that a smoothly muscled back that held remnants of a tan.

Unable to take her eyes from that back, Faith took in a quick breath and sat up. She clutched the sheet to her breasts and swallowed once, hard. That was all it took for the events of the night before to slowly begin to filter through the fog that still clouded her brain.

"Sawyer?" she called in a very low, very shaky voice. The second time around, she managed to make it a little louder, but no less shaky. "Sawyer?"

He didn't move. For a split second she wondered whether it wasn't Sawyer after all but a big dummy he'd left as a joke. She'd like that. She'd like the things—pictures, images, flashes of memory—from the night before to have been make-believe.

But no. That was real live flesh, real live Sawyer Bell, real live *naked* Sawyer Bell beside her.

"Sawyer?" she called, this time in a panic. "Sawyer!"

He jerked, then groaned and put a hand on the side of his head.

"Sawyer, get up!" Tugging the top sheet free of the quilt, she scrambled to the side of the bed and wrapped it around her as she stood. When she looked back at Sawyer, he was rolling onto his back. "Get up, Sawyer. Oh please, get up."

He opened his eyes a crack, much as she'd done not so long before. As she'd done, he squeezed them tight again. But Faith wasn't allowing him the leisure she'd had to let memory come calling. "Sawyer." He grunted. "Sawyer!"

He pried his eyes open and focused on her, and for a minute he simply stared, trying without success to make sense out of what he was seeing. Finally he frowned. "Faith?" He knew it had to be her. There wasn't anyone who had quite her face, quite her hair, quite her voice. But he had no idea what she could possibly be doing standing by the side of his bed draped in a sheet.

Then he realized that the setting was wrong. Moving his head by short, pained inches, he saw that he wasn't in his own bedroom at all. His bedroom was done in navies and browns. This one was heavy on whites and hurt his eyes something awful. And the bed was too small. His heel was caught on the bottom edge of the mattress. That never happened with his extra-long king. And he would never, *never* sleep on flowered sheets under a flowered quilt, but unless his eyesight was truly going, that was what he saw above and below his hip. His *naked* hip.

Bolting upright, he winced and caught himself for a minute, then grabbed the quilt from the bed and, though he was plenty warm on his own, wrapped it around him as he hurried to stand on the opposite side of the mattress from Faith. Memory was fast returning, coming in flashes like a strobe tormenting his brain.

"What happened?" he rasped. He hoped she'd tell him that he'd simply had too much to drink, so she'd put him to bed. Somehow, between the look on her face and the images that were flashing in his mind, he doubted that was the case.

"We did it," she whispered in dismay. Then she paused and allowed herself a last-ditch doubt. "Did we?"

Sawyer looked down at the bed. They'd just awoken in it. Clearly they'd spent at least part of the night here. But the pictures flickering into his mind were of someplace darker, like the living room, and someplace harder, like the floor. "Do you see any clothes?" he asked cautiously. He didn't. There was nothing draped over the white wicker chair in the corner, nothing thrown on the white wicker dresser, nothing dropped on the pale green carpet.

"No. I think they may be, uh, in the other room."

Sawyer's headache gave an extra-strong pulse as though in punishment for what the evidence was strongly suggesting. He raked a hand through his hair. "Were we drunk?"

"I don't know. I've never been drunk before. Do you remember much?"

"Bits and pieces."

"Did we...?"

Sawyer tuned into several of those bits and pieces. He remembered talking about Joanna but seeing Faith. He remembered touching her. He remembered that she felt very good to hold. He remembered that she was very tight inside. "I think so."

"Oh Lord." She twisted down onto the bed, putting her back to him, which gave her a token protection from the embarrassment she felt. She rested her splitting head in her hands. "Oh Lord. I've never, *never* done anything like this. I'm sorry, Sawyer."

"It was my fault as much as yours," he snapped.

She hunched her shoulders. "No need to be snippy about it."

He rubbed a hand over his eyes and was a while in answering. "Sorry."

"Are you always this charming when you wake up?"

"I'm not feeling great. Everything from my neck up is hurting. Even my tongue doesn't feel right."

"Maybe it overexerted itself."

"Look who's being snippy."

For a minute, she sat in quiet dejection. Then she shook her head—which was a mistake. Everything inside seemed to rattle. After another minute's recovery, she said, "I guess I was trying to be cute, only it didn't work." She closed her eyes and whispered, "I don't believe this." Her voice rose. "I don't believe I let all that happen. *Let* it happen. I did it. I goaded you on. I know I did. Why did I do that? I've never been sexually aggressive in my life!"

"You'd had too much to drink. We'd both had too much to drink. Neither of us was thinking clearly."

"But to—make—love." She tripped over the words, as though the sound of them hitting the air made the fact of what they'd done so much more real. "Making love is the most intimate thing two people can do. But we're not lovers, you and me," she cried. "We're friends!"

Sawyer winced. "You don't have to yell."

"We're friends," she repeated, but more softly.

"Some say that friends make the best lovers."

"Or that the best of friendships are ruined when friends become lovers. I don't want that to happen, Sawyer." She swore softly. "I don't believe this."

"We were tipsy."

"We were awful. Some of the things we said. What we did to Jack and Joanna. That was the *lowest*. Who are we to go on and on about them that way? To talk about the way they made love?" She buried her face in her hands and moaned. "I am so embarrassed."

"We were tipsy."

"They didn't deserve that. Do you think they're off with new lovers, talking about what *we* did in bed? I'd die if I knew Jack was doing that. Some things are sacred." She made a snorting sound. "Boy, we blew sacred, didn't we?"

"The problem is that I know Jack and you know

Joanna. We used to go places, the four of us. It's almost natural that we make comparisons.''

"It's terrible! How can you condone what we did?"

"I'm not condoning it. But we were tipsy."

"I *know* we were tipsy, still what we did was awful!"

"I know." He held his head. "I take that back. I don't know. Things are coming back to me, and some of them are pretty nice."

Faith whirled on him, but the sudden movement wrenched everything inside her. For a split second she feared she was going to be sick. Mercifully the feeling passed. "I think," she said with her eyes lowered, "that I'd like something for this headache and then a cup or two of very strong coffee."

Both ideas sounded good to Sawyer. He didn't move, though. He didn't want to do anything to anger Faith. She wasn't in the best of moods and neither was he. So he watched her walk from the bedroom with surprising grace, given that she was swathed in a bedsheet. He saw her go into the bathroom and shut the door. It seemed forever that she was in there. He began to wonder whether she was all right, but he didn't move. He simply stood by the side of the bed, holding the flowered quilt wrapped around his lower half.

Finally the door opened and she came out. He guessed she'd thrown water on her face and brushed her hair, because she looked a little more awake. She was also wearing a robe.

"Here," she said quietly. Keeping her eyes low—
in deference to her headache rather than deference to
him, he was sure—she dropped several tablets into
his hand. Then she turned and, walking gingerly,
headed for the kitchen.

As soon as she'd disappeared, he took his pain-
staking turn in the bathroom. When he joined her in
the kitchen a short time later, he was wearing the
sweatshirt and jeans he'd recovered, with more than
a little chagrin, from the living-room floor.

The smell of perking coffee wafted about and
would have been welcoming if Faith hadn't been
standing so still, facing the counter, keeping her back
to him. He slipped onto a bar stool. His legs weren't
feeling as steady as usual. The support was welcome.

As he sat there, waiting for the pills to calm the
noise in his head and take the raw edge off everything
else, he wondered if Faith wanted him to leave. She
had every right to be alone if she wanted. It was her
house. She wasn't feeling well, and his presence was
a reminder why.

But he couldn't leave. The cold water he'd doused
his head with in the sink had cleared his mind that
much. He and Faith had to talk.

He didn't do a thing, though, until the coffee was
done and she handed him a steaming mug. He'd always thought of life as being more civilized over
morning coffee, and Faith's coffee was strong. If it
didn't make him more civilized, he didn't know what
would. He figured it would also go a long way toward
settling his stomach and dulling the ache in his head.

It did both for Faith. After a few minutes, she was able to carry her mug to the counter, take the companion stool to his and face him. "Guess we missed dinner," she said. She was relieved to see that his eyes had the same sickly red look hers did.

"Guess so."

"If we'd had something in our stomachs, the champagne wouldn't have hit so hard."

"Either that, or we'd have been bounced from the restaurant."

She started to smile at that thought, but the movement of her mouth somehow reached her eyes, which still hurt. So she made a quiet sound to acknowledge what he'd said and closed her eyes for a minute. "I feel very foolish," she whispered.

"That's two of us."

"I have never, *never* done anything like this before. I mean, even aside from what we did to Jack and Joanna, the sex was something else." She opened her eyes to his. "I don't sleep around, Sawyer. I never have. There was one guy before I met Jack, and there haven't been any since. Except you."

Sawyer thought about that for a minute. "I'm flattered."

"I didn't mean it as flattery. I meant it to tell you the way I am. I'm not loose. I'm not a frustrated divorcée. I don't go around getting drunk and begging men to make love to me."

"Is that what you thought you did?"

"Yes."

"Well, you didn't. In the first place, you didn't get

drunk. If you'd done that, you'd have been incapacitated. You'd probably have passed out. Neither of us was drunk. We were tipsy. That's all."

"Is there really a difference?" she asked.

The faint bitterness in her voice annoyed him. "Yes, there is," he insisted. "There's a big difference. If we'd been drunk we wouldn't have been so lucid."

"Lucid? You think we were lucid?"

"To some extent, yes. The things I said about Joanna were true. I probably shouldn't have said any of them. But they were true. She did a job on me sexually. There were times when I wondered whether I lacked something in that department, since I couldn't make her respond. I never would have planned what happened last night, but once we got going I must have had an inner need to keep going. You were my friend. I'd had just enough to drink. I was loose. I wanted to know if I could turn you on. So maybe I used bad judgment, and I blame that on the drink, but on some level I knew what I was doing." He paused. "My guess is you did, too."

Faith let his words sink in. Much as she tried, she couldn't completely deny them. Quietly she said, "Then we have to accept the responsibility. So that makes it worse."

"Yes and no."

She stared at him. "Explain."

"Yes, we have to accept the responsibility. We're mature adults. We can blame what we did on the wine, but that doesn't excuse it. On the other hand, maybe it wasn't so terrible."

"Are you kidding?" she cried. "Sawyer, we slept together last night! You and me. Best friends. Best buddies. We made love. We went all the way. We scr—"

He cut her off. "Don't say it, Faith. Don't even think it. You're right. We're best friends. Best buddies. We shouldn't have done what we did, but it wasn't some ugly, faceless, nameless thing, and I'm sure as hell not dropping a C-note on your counter and walking out."

Faith flinched. She bowed her head and pressed two fingers to her temple. Feeling quickly contrite, Sawyer gentled his voice. "All I'm saying is that this isn't the end of the world."

"What if I'm pregnant?"

The thought caught him off guard. He swallowed. "Is there a chance of that?"

"Yes. I don't use birth control. I haven't had any need." She grew defensive. "I don't go around doing this kind of thing."

Rattled as he was, her defensiveness hit him the wrong way. "Damn it, I know that, Faith! Will you stop saying it? I *know* you're not loose. I *know* you don't sleep around. I *know* you place value on physical intimacy. We may never have been romantically involved, but I do know you, and better than most, I'd wager."

"You must think I'm awful."

He threw his hands in the air; they came down on his hips. "It takes two to tango, y'know."

"But I kept pushing you on. I kept asking you for more." Her eyes grew moist. "I swear, Sawyer, I've never been like that before."

The tears did it. He'd had no intention of touching her, but when he saw the tears he couldn't sit by and stay physically aloof. Not after what, right or wrong, they'd done. And not when every one of his instincts as a friend and as a man directed him otherwise.

Taking a step to her stool, he wrapped his arms around her. "I want you to listen to me, Faith. You're a bright woman, probably one of the brightest I've ever met. I want you to listen and listen good. Okay?"

She nodded.

He spoke slowly, keeping his voice low and gentle. "I do not think less of you for what we did last night. If anything, the opposite is true. I'm flattered to know that there haven't been any other men but that you let me be the first since the divorce. I'm relieved to know that you're human, that deep down inside you have some of the same needs as me—even if the need is as lousy as criticizing our ex-spouses. I am not disappointed in you. I don't think I could ever be disappointed in you." He paused. "How can I be disappointed when you came so alive in my arms?"

"Sawyer," she moaned.

"Okay. We won't talk about that."

"Don't even *think* about it."

"Fine. What about your being pregnant? When will you know?"

"Two weeks, give or take."

"Then we won't think about that, either, until we know one way or another. There's no point in worrying, and there's no way we can change the chances. If it happened, it's already happened, and if that's the case, we'll sit down together and decide what to do."

Faith couldn't fault his logic. But then, she'd always found Sawyer to be logical. She'd always thought she was, too, which was why she was surprised by her own heightened emotions.

"Sound fair?" he asked, when she remained quiet in his arms.

She nodded. "What do we do in the meantime?"

It was a little while before he answered. He honestly didn't know what to do. "Maybe we ought to go on the way we always have."

"Business as usual?"

"That's right."

"There's only one problem with that. Business as usual means running into each other only by accident. But there's the little matter of the Leindecker divorce."

"The Leindecker divorce."

"Remember? The thing that brought you down to my office in the first place yesterday?"

"I remember." But he hadn't until then, and the recollection gave greater weight to what had happened in the intervening hours. "Oh boy."

Faith knew what he was thinking. "Uh-huh. If we

were wondering whether there was a conflict of interest *then*, what's the story *now*?"

Reluctantly Sawyer let his arms fall from around her. He sank back onto his stool. "No different, I guess. We're still okay as long as we watch what we do."

"You can pretend last night didn't happen?"

"No. But I don't know if it'll happen again, and if it doesn't, not much has really changed." He paused. "Has it?"

"I guess not."

"Do you feel that because of last night you'll be less strong an advocate for your client?"

"I don't know. Maybe I won't be as tough a negotiator knowing I'm negotiating with you."

Sawyer narrowed his eyes, which were beginning to feel better. "You'll be tough. Probably more so than usual, if for no other reason than to make the point that you aren't biased by any relationship with me. Of course," he mused, "if you feel uncomfortable about it, you can tell Mrs. Leindecker to get another lawyer."

Faith smirked. "Would that please you?"

"No way. I said I was excited about working with you. I was simply considering your feelings."

"If you're that considerate, you could always withdraw from the case yourself. You could tell Mr. Leindecker to get another lawyer."

"But I want to work with you."

"Against me."

"Against you. It's a challenge, and in that sense both of our clients stand to benefit."

At that moment, Faith wasn't much up for challenges. But in an hour, a day, a week, things would be different. She'd been accepting challenges since she first applied to law school. Fighting prejudice, she'd had to work twice as hard because she was female, but she'd proven herself every bit as good a lawyer as any other she'd run across.

"A woman in Mrs. Leindecker's position deserves the best if she's going to get the respect she's earned," she told him.

"A man in Mr. Leindecker's position *needs* the best if he doesn't want to be taken to the cleaners."

"They were married a long time," she warned. "She's put up with a lot."

"She's *had* a lot. She's lived like a queen."

"Which is how she deserves to be kept. You can't just expect her to go off, get a job and live hand-to-mouth all of a sudden, do you?"

"Come on, Faith. It's not like she's got little kids to take care of—or that she's doddering at the older end of the scale. She's a healthy, middle-aged woman. It wouldn't kill her to work."

"What could she do? She's not trained for anything. Any job she'd get would pay her a fraction of what your client earns. We're talking the most menial, entry-level position if she had to work. But she shouldn't have to. Not if he led her to believe that she'd always be taken care of. There are things like service and loyalty and unspoken contracts to consider.''

"Tell it to the judge.''

There it was, Faith knew. The gauntlet had been thrown down. And Sawyer Bell was looking at her with a crooked half-grin on his handsome face, waiting, just waiting to see if she had the courage to pick it up.

She wasn't sure whether it was the grin, the handsome face, the need to put last night's folly behind them or the challenge itself that did it. But she rose from the stool, tipped up her chin and informed him in slow, clear words, "I intend to, thank you."

With that, she reached for the refrigerator door.

4

Faith made a huge breakfast, not so much because Sawyer might be hungry, but because she was. Then, trying to pretend that nothing out of the ordinary had happened between them, she sent him on his way.

Saturdays were work days. On this particular one, she had to go to the grocery for food, the dry cleaner for a drop-off and pickup, the department store for stockings and a refill of mascara. Despite the aspirin, the coffee and the breakfast, she was still feeling a little logy. But she pushed herself. There were things to be done, and if she didn't grab the opportunity, she'd lose it.

She had to smile at that thought; it was the credo by which Jack lived. Over and over he'd said those words during the eight years they'd been married—usually at times when Faith was at her laziest. Since the divorce she'd been more diligent about all those non-law-related things that she would have let ride in the past. Without Jack to keep her on her toes, she had to rely on herself.

So he wasn't all bad, she told herself and knew that it was a way of compensating for how she'd belittled him with Sawyer. In honor of Jack, she even went shopping for a new suit for work, one that was conservative and practical like him, and though she'd probably have picked something more daring on another day, she knew she'd wear it well.

By the time she returned to Union Wharf it was nearly three in the afternoon. Curled up on the sofa in deliberate defiance of what had happened behind it the night before, she spent several hours making notes on a case that would be coming up for a hearing that week. Then she slipped into a sexy black sheath, made good use of the eye makeup she'd just happened to buy along with the mascara that afternoon, and went to a harvest party at Monica's home in Concord.

The best part, she decided, was the drive to and from Concord. Faith enjoyed driving. She didn't do it often, since she usually walked to and from work, but when she had a case in one of the outlying courthouses, or when she found something to do on a weekend that took her out of the city, she drove with relish. She tuned the radio to her favorite station, the only one in Boston that played country music, and she relaxed. She beat her left foot in time to the music, clapped her hands when a traffic light freed them, hummed along from time to time, even sang aloud when a particular lyric grabbed her.

Monica's party, on the other hand, was a drag. Not that Monica hadn't warned her. Most of the guests were friends of Monica's husband, who was fifteen years older than Monica, who was ten years older than Faith. If those guests had been lawyers, Faith might have had a chance, but the men were in business, and their wives were professional wives. Faith couldn't identify with them at all.

Oh, she managed. She was adept at small talk. Sipping her customary Perrier and lime, she did her share of chatting about the weather, the turn of the leaves, the new musical that had opened at the Shubert, a recently published novel that had the city talking. She listened in on business discussions, knowing that the small bits of information she picked up would come in handy at one point or another in her life. But the talk didn't excite her. There was nothing lively about the gathering. None of the people made her laugh in delight, and if a party wasn't for laughing in delight, Faith didn't know what it *was* for. For Monica's sake, though, she stuck it out.

She liked Monica. She also respected her. Monica had started out being like the other women at the party, but it hadn't taken her long to realize that if her marriage was to have any chance of survival, she needed something constructive to do. Fortunately her husband understood. He put her through law school and indulged her through ten years of work as a public defender. That was what she was doing when Faith met her. When Faith had decided to leave the law firm she was associated with and go out on her own, Monica was ready for a move.

For five years, they had been splitting the rent on their suite of offices and sharing Loni's salary and skills. Though they often discussed legal issues with each other, their practices were entirely independent. Outside the office, they were friends.

So when, as a friend, Monica had pleaded with Faith to come liven up her husband's party, Faith had agreed. Unfortunately the party needed a kind of livening that Faith, despite her intelligence and quick wit, couldn't begin to accomplish. Still, Faith wasn't sorry she went. The party wasn't a waste. It took up four hours. By the time she drove back into the city, parked her car and safely locked herself into her condo, she was exhausted enough to go straight to sleep.

Unfortunately she'd made a large tactical error. In keeping with the schedule she stuck to in her post-Jack life, she had done no more than make her bed that morning. Sundays were for changing the sheets.

This week, she should have changed them on Saturday. Though she'd aired the bed as always, neatly made it and fluffed the pillows, and though she was tired enough to fall asleep soon after she crawled in, she awoke at four in the morning thinking Sawyer was beside her. And no wonder. The scent of him clung to her sheets. It was so subtle that she wondered at first whether she was imagining it, but the warmth of her body had brought it to life, and she wasn't able to ignore it.

She tried. She tried doing what she'd done all of Saturday, keeping her mind busy enough so that there wasn't room for a wayward thought. But at four in the morning, she couldn't manufacture distractions.

There were just the lingering lights of the harbor, the sleeping city, the night and Sawyer.

For the first time, perhaps the very first time since she'd known the man, she allowed herself to take a long, objective look at him physically. It wasn't hard. She might not have thought to heed the details before, still they'd registered. Her mind's eye held an exquisitely detailed picture of him.

He was tall, she guessed six-four or six-five. He'd played basketball in college, she knew because he'd mentioned it once, and though the injuries he sustained in Vietnam had dashed any hopes of a professional career, he still had the body of an athlete. He *was* an athlete. A runner. He'd pushed himself and pushed himself, well beyond the point his doctors had ever thought he'd be able to go, which was a testimony to his will...and to Joanna's, Faith freely admitted. Despite the scars that he'd always carry, he had full command of his body to do with as he pleased.

He was broad-shouldered and narrow-hipped, both of which she'd known forever, neither of which she'd appreciated quite as fully as she had the night before. Though she only remembered seeing his upper body naked, she remembered measuring those parts of him below the waist with her hands. Narrow-hipped, he was, indeed, with legs that could wind forever in and round her own.

Taking in a sharp breath, she put a hand to her chest to calm the wild beat of her heart. But the warmth of her palm served only to remind her of the warmth of Sawyer's hands on her skin. Oh, yes, his hands were warm. They were large and well formed, both strong and gentle.

That was pretty much the way she saw his face, too. Strong but gentle, dark but giving, sober but capable of a buoyant smile. His hair was dark brown and stylishly worn, tumbling over his brow with the least encouragement, and his skin never quite looked as pale as the rest of the world's. There was a ruddiness to it. Like a child, his color heightened with exertion or excitement—or passion, she thought, though she had no way of knowing for sure. It had been too dark in their nook behind the sofa last night to see that.

What she had seen, or felt, was the prickle of his beard. That, too, gave his face a darker, more rugged look, and though she'd never seen him with enough stubble to be called grubby, many times she'd seen a distinct five o'clock shadow. She hadn't thought twice about it before. Now she did, and she decided that it added to the aura of masculinity that surrounded him.

Which was a whole new thought, in itself. Aura of masculinity? He did have that, and he had it in abundance. But she'd never noticed it before, and she couldn't understand why. Surely something that hit her so strongly now had to have hit her on some level before. Maybe, she mused, she'd repressed it. That was an interesting thought.

As she wrestled with it, she could almost see Sawyer standing back, finding a wry humor in her predicament. She could see his brown eyes twinkling, could see his firm mouth twitching at the corners, could even see one dark eyebrow edging upward into an arch. She tried to be annoyed with him, as he stood there in her mind, but she couldn't. He was a good man. And he was gorgeous.

Uh-huh. Gorgeous. He was. But that didn't change the fact that they were best of friends, had no intention of being involved with each other as lovers, had no *business* being intimately involved if they intended to represent the Leindeckers. And yes, if Laura Leindecker decided to go ahead with the divorce, Faith was in it on her side. In spite of what had happened the night before, she couldn't turn down the golden opportunity of seeing how Sawyer Bell worked.

Faith started Sunday by listing the things she wanted to do. She made it halfway down the list— changing the sheets, doing the laundry, poring through the Sunday *Globe* right down to the cross-word puzzle at the back of the magazine section— before Sawyer called.

She recognized his voice at once. It might have been the deep timbre, she mused, or the faint hesitance, or she had to admit that, as much as she busied her mind, Sawyer was still a presence in it. She wasn't sure whether to be pleased he'd called or not, and for that reason she attributed the pickup of her pulse to uncertainty.

"I just wanted to make sure you were okay," he explained in a still-hesitant but gentle and sincere tone. "Somehow it didn't seem right to leave yesterday and not be in touch for days."

She agreed with him and was touched, though not entirely surprised. Sawyer was a considerate man. "Thank you. I'm doing fine." She laughed softly. "I feel a lot better today then I did yesterday. I can move my eyes."

"Mmm. Me, too. After I left you, I came home and slept. Slept on and off for the rest of the day. I've never been hit quite like that."

"You must have been tired anyway."

"Maybe. Still, I don't think I'm ever having another drink."

"Uh-huh," she said, not believing it for a minute.

"I'm serious."

"I'm sure you are. But the holiday season is coming. There are lots of dinners and parties. One drink won't kill you."

"The second or third might."

"Mmm." She thought back to Dewey O'Day's affair. "Why did we do that, Sawyer? Why did we keep taking wine from the tray?"

"We were bored. We didn't want to be there."

"We were laughing a lot. We weren't keeping count of what we had to drink."

"We were giving each other courage. Boy, were we dumb."

"You can say that again."

"Once is enough, thanks. I usually try to be more responsible than we were that night." He paused. "At least we didn't make fools of ourselves at the party."

"The party wasn't the problem. It was all we had to drink after that."

"But if we hadn't drunk what we did at the party, we'd have been more clearheaded afterward. I'd have known not to open that bottle of wine at my place, and you'd have saved the Johnsons' champagne for a better occasion. Now it's gone."

"No loss. Besides, I wasn't about to drink that champagne all alone, and if I was going to share it with someone, who better than you? You're a friend."

"Am I still?" he asked. The hesitancy she'd heard earlier, gone for a while, was back.

"Of course, you are."

"Even though I took advantage of you?"

Faith sighed indulgently. "Sawyer, you didn't take advantage of me. I asked for everything I got. And no one forced me to take out that champagne."

"But I'm bigger than you."

She didn't see the connection. He hadn't used physical force. She doubted he was capable of it where a woman was concerned. "So?"

"So I should have been able to hold my liquor better. I should have been that much more sober than you every step of the way."

"You're wallowing in guilt. Oh boy, are you wallowing."

"Damn right, I am."

"Well, don't. Because if you do, I'll have to. You say you should have been stronger physically, I say I should have been stronger mentally."

"Mentally?"

"I should have said no. Traditionally the woman is the one who has a saner head on her shoulders. I should have refused another drink the minute I knew I wasn't in total control."

"But you weren't in total control, which is why you did what you did."

"Even in *partial* control, I should have known better." She stopped for a minute to think about what they were saying. "This goes round and round, doesn't it?"

"Yeah. I thought we'd agreed—" there was a break in the transmission of his voice "—the blame—hell, my time's up. I don't have any more change."

"Change?" Apparently, he was calling from a pay phone. "Where are you?"

"The Cape. I bought a dilapidated—" there was another break "—summer—I'm fixing it up. Gotta run, Faith. Are you sure you're okay?"

"I'm fine."

"Talk with you soon, then. Bye."

He broke the connection before she could say another word. She pictured him dashing out of the phone booth before the operator could ring to tell him that he owed another quarter for the extra seconds he'd used. The image brought a smile to her face. He really was adorable. And admirable. So he'd bought a dilapidated something on the Cape and was fixing it up. Physical work on the weekends to balance the cerebral work of the week. He was a bright man, indeed.

Several hours later, she was wishing she had some physical work of her own to do. Having finished the crossword puzzle down to the very last word, she was reading through some papers for work. But she felt restless. She wanted to be out doing something, though she didn't have any idea what that something might be. She thought of taking a walk, but the day was gray and not particularly enticing. She thought of calling a friend and going to a movie, but there wasn't one that she desperately wanted to see. She thought of calling a friend, period, but that would mean chatting about personal things, and she wasn't in the mood for that, either.

When Laura Leindecker's daughter called her on the phone, she welcomed the diversion.

"I'm sorry to bother you, Ms Barry, but Mother said you were representing her, and I had to talk with someone."

"Actually," Faith tried to explain, "your mother and I haven't any formal agreement yet. She was going to take a few days to decide whether she really wants to go ahead with the divorce."

"I think she does," came the answering voice, soft, like her mother's, but more high-pitched. "And I think she should. Especially after what's happened this weekend."

"What is that?"

"He's been here at the house since noon yesterday, and he refuses to leave. The more Mother asks him, the more belligerent he becomes."

"Belligerent?" According to Laura, the man had been charming and humble.

"Yes, belligerent. Please. Let me talk with you. I'm taking a six o'clock flight back to Baltimore tonight, but I could meet you at your office—or anywhere else in Boston before that. I want you to hear my side of the story."

"The divorce," Faith reminded her gently, "is between your parents. Shouldn't your mother be telling me whatever there is to tell?"

"She's too...timid sometimes. I don't know how much she'll tell. But she's suffering, and I think you should know the facts. They could come in handy when you're planning her case."

Faith couldn't deny the temptation of facts. She knew she'd have to decide whether what she was told was, indeed, factual, but she felt she owed it to her client to listen. So she gave Beth Leindecker directions to her office and agreed to meet her there at four.

Beth, it turned out, was twenty-three, an intern at an ad agency and definitely at odds with her father. "When I arrived home on Friday night, Mother was distraught."

"Did you see or speak with your father that night?"

"No. Mother told him to sleep somewhere else. For all we know, he slept with *her*."

"Do you know who she is?"

"I didn't even know she existed until Mother called on Friday morning!"

Faith wondered whether that call had come before or after Laura's confrontation with her husband. It would be interesting to know how much Beth was egging her on. "Okay. So your father came to the house on Saturday morning."

"Around noon. We couldn't believe he dared show his face there."

"It's still his home."

"But he's not welcome there."

Faith was tempted to point out a few basic legal facts to Beth. Instead, she said, "He must have needed clothes. Grooming things."

"That was what we thought, but he wasn't back for those at all. He was back to stay, he said. He said that the whole thing had gotten out of hand, that Mother had blown it out of proportion. Can you believe that? He admits to cheating on her, then tells her she's blown it out of proportion!"

Faith held up an appeasing hand. In some ways, Beth sounded just like her mother—but with a hotter spark and a shorter fuse. "You mentioned belligerence," she prompted to keep the girl on track.

Beth nodded. "They were arguing back and forth. He was saying that what he did wasn't so awful, and Mother was saying that it was, and I agreed with her."

"You were standing right there in the middle of the fight?"

"I had to. Someone had to protect Mother."

"She couldn't protect herself?"

"Not against him. She's never been able to protect herself against him. He snaps his fingers, and she comes running. It's always been that way."

"Maybe she loves him."

Beth's only response to that was a frown. "She doesn't deserve this hurt. After all these years, she deserves some satisfaction."

"What kind of satisfaction did you have in mind?" Faith asked, genuinely curious.

"He ought to be banned from stepping foot in that house or coming near my mother. She's had a lifetime of his harassment."

"Harassment." Faith echoed the word. It didn't fit with the image Laura had painted of her husband any more than belligerence did. "Harassment by omission, as in emotional neglect?"

"For years it was that. Now it's physical. He started throwing things."

Faith grew more alert. "What kinds of things?"

"The mail, first. Letters and magazines that were on the table in the front hall. Then towels that were piled on the stairs. Then flowers that were on a table at the top of the stairs. Then books, big books from the nightstand."

"The argument worked its way to their bedroom?"

"He followed her there. She kept yelling at him, telling him to stay away, but he followed her there."

"Did he hit her at any point?"

"No."

"At any point, did he raise a hand to strike her?"

"No," Beth said, and Faith sensed a reluctance in the denial. Beth was clearly eager to think the worst of her father.

"He was just throwing things around. Anything bigger than a book?"

"He kicked the cushion off the chaise lounge. It went halfway across the room."

"Did he aim it at her?"

"No."

"Did he aim anything directly at her?"

"No. But you're missing the point," Beth insisted. "He was throwing things. She could have been hit."

Faith was quiet for several minutes, trying to put what Beth was saying in some kind of perspective, enough to decide whether there was any cause for immediate concern. "That was yesterday afternoon. I take it he's calmed down since then."

"He's still there. She wants him out."

Does she, or do you? Faith was wondering. "Has he calmed down?"

"Yes. But he's still angry. He could act up again at any time." Beth looked truly frustrated. "For the first time in her life, my mother is standing up to him. At least, she's trying to. But if someone doesn't give her a boost, she's going to fall right back on him. I think you should give her that boost, Ms Barry."

Faith didn't like the sound of that at all, and it wasn't because she lacked the courage for it. "Morally, I'm obliged to see if the marriage can be salvaged. I can't urge your mother to push for a divorce. It has to be her decision. If she gives it fair thought, decides that there's no hope for the marriage and that divorce is the only solution, I'll help her. I'm not sure what else I can do. I'll call her, if that will make you feel better. I'll ask how she feels about his being around. There are many couples who live together right up to the point of signing a legal separation agreement. It's sometimes simpler that way. Then again, if your mother is being physically threatened, that's another story."

"She is."

"I'll ask her about it," Faith said, and rose from her desk. "In the meantime, I think you'd be best not goading her on. Be supportive. But remember that this is between your parents. You're grown and out of the house. They have to come to terms with what they want from each other for the next however many years."

Beth took up her overnight case and started for the door. "I think mother needs a court order to keep him out of the house."

"Be supportive, Beth, not inflammatory."

"She needs someone to light a fire under her."

"Do you hate your father that much?"

"I don't hate him."

"Then why are you so eager to get him out of the house?"

"He needs to be taught a lesson. He's had everything his way for so long. It's fine and dandy for him to be delightfully pleasant when he's pulling all the strings. Let someone else pull the strings and he starts throwing things the way he did Saturday. That was an awakening, let me tell you.''

''That he has a temper?''

''I'll say.''

''Maybe it's a healthy outlet. After all, he was objecting to his wife's kicking him out of the house. Maybe he really wants to be there with her.''

''He just wants his way.''

''Maybe,'' Faith conceded, then smiled and squeezed the younger woman's shoulder. ''Have a safe flight back to Baltimore. And remember, stay cool. Your parents are going to have to work this out themselves.''

''Will you call my mother?''

''As soon as you're on your way.''

But she'd barely seen Beth to the elevator and returned to her office when Laura called her. ''Is Beth still there? I know she was going to meet you. Has she left?''

''Just a minute ago. Is there a problem?''

''She forgot her gray outfit, the two-piece wool she wore in on Friday. She was too warm in it then, but the weather's getting colder and she'll want it.'' She sighed. ''It's no wonder she forgot it. She was in such a stir while she was here.''

''Has she always had trouble getting along with her father?''

''Always. I've been the buffer for years. She feels that he's been unduly stingy with her.''

''With money?''

''Money, time, himself. He said it would be too

easy to spoil her, and he didn't want that. God forbid he should make things easy for her. When she graduated from college, she wanted to work for him, but he told her she had to work somewhere else. 'Earn her stripes' was the expression he used. What kind of father would make his daughter do that?''

''Many have.''

''It was very selfish of him. But I suppose that's nothing new,'' Laura concluded sadly.

Faith heard the sadness. She didn't hear any sort of panic. ''Beth was concerned for your physical safety. Are you all right?''

''I'm fine. Bruce is being difficult, of course. He insists on staying here. When I tell him to leave, he gets furious.''

''Do you feel that you're in danger?''

''I don't know what he's going to do next. I've never seen him like this.''

''Has he threatened you in any way? Forced you in any physical sense?''

''No. But one of us has to leave this house, and it isn't going to be me. *He* can leave.''

''It sounds as if he won't. We can try for a restraining order, but it may be premature.'' While Faith was the first one to want to protect a client from physical harm, she sensed that the threat in this case was more speculative than real. Bruce had no history of violence. The court would see that. ''I'd recommend that you take advantage of his presence and talk with him.''

''Talk? What for? I can't trust what he says. Not

anymore. Besides, it's a waste of time. I want a divorce.''

"I understand that, Mrs. Leindecker, but—"

"I want a divorce. Are you going to represent me?"

"Let's discuss that on Tuesday."

"This is Sunday. My feelings won't change in two days."

"Where emotions are concerned, a lot can happen in two days."

"Not in my case. I want a divorce, and the sooner we get started, the sooner that man will see what he's done."

Divorce for the purpose of revenge was one of the things Faith least liked. It was childish, blind and often ugly. It also tended to overshadow any pluses that might have existed in a marriage. Gut instinct told her that this marriage had pluses aplenty. What she needed was time to see if those pluses could possibly reassert themselves.

"Tuesday, Laura. We'll talk again on Tuesday."

It took another minute, but she finally convinced Laura to hold off any action until then. Hanging up the phone at last, she quickly gathered her things together and left the office. She wasn't as easily able to leave behind thoughts of the case. It bothered her. Clearly, emotions were flying high in the Leindecker home. But a divorce based solely on emotional factors was the most painful for all involved, including the lawyers. Granted, any divorce stirred emotions. At some point, though, practicality and reason had to come into play. It could happen in court. Or before. Faith far preferred the latter.

Letting herself into her apartment, she had a sudden urge to phone Sawyer. She had a good excuse. Her client had called her in fear; Faith was sharing that fear with the lawyer who might, with a call to his client, be able to help.

But Sawyer wasn't home. He'd called her from the Cape—she didn't even know where on the Cape. And he'd called from a pay phone, which meant that the dilapidated something he'd bought didn't have one of its own.

Just for the hell of it, she tried his number in Boston. After ten rings without an answer, she hung up. She told herself that that was okay, that she really didn't have to speak with him, that Laura Leindecker was perfectly safe. But an hour later, she tried again, and then again an hour after that. It was ten o'clock before she finally reached him.

5

"Hi, Sawyer, it's me."

She was the last person he'd expected to hear from, still he recognized her voice at once. "Faith?"

"Uh-huh. I've been trying you. You must have just come home."

"There was an accident on the Sagamore Bridge that backed traffic up for miles. I thought it was late enough in the season for the crowds to be gone, but I sat in the middle of a jam for three hours."

She knew how frustrating that could be and would have felt sorry for him if she weren't so envious that he'd been at the Cape in the first place. "Tell me again what you were doing down there."

"I bought a place this summer. It's in East Dennis, an old broken-down thing. But it's on a lake, and it has potential. The land is gorgeous. I figured I could fix up the place myself. I'm an experienced man when it comes to repairs."

The way he drawled it made her smile. "The house in Cambridge?"

"Yeah. Then it was physical therapy more than anything. I suppose it's still that. The physical exercise is different from what I do at work all week. But it's also mentally therapeutic. Gets out the cobwebs, if you know what I mean." He wasn't sure she did. He wasn't sure she'd been thinking of him as much as he'd been thinking of her. They'd agreed to go back to business as usual. But he was having trouble doing that. Maybe the fact that she'd called him meant she was having trouble with it, too.

"Tell me about this place," she said. "How much land do you have?"

"Three acres."

"So you don't see your neighbors?"

"Nope. All I see is trees. And water. And rabbits and raccoons and geese. It's such a total change from everything I have up here—including the house. I mean, we're talking old and worn and crumbly."

"Sounds like you might want to tear it down and start over from scratch."

That thought had occurred to him. "The problem is I'm already committed. The deeper in I get, the more I find that needs to be done, but the more I've done, the less I want to ditch the whole thing." He paused. "Am I making any sense?"

"Lots of it," she said. "You've committed yourself to a course of action. You've come too far to turn back."

"Oh, I'm not sure *too* far," he drawled. "I'm still debating."

"But you keep going back, and you keep doing work, and you keep getting deeper involved."

"Like I say, it's therapeutic."

"Which means that if you finally decide to ditch

the project, you'll still have gotten something out of it.''

''That's one way of looking at it. You're good at rationalizing, Faith.''

''Sometimes,'' she said. She was thinking of what they'd done with each other on Friday night. She couldn't rationalize it away so easily. Nor, much as she tried, could she forget it for long. But that was beside the point. ''I have to ask your opinion on something, Sawyer.''

''Shoot.''

''Bruce Leindecker. Do you know him well?''

''Well enough,'' he answered more cautiously. ''We've been passing acquaintances for several years.''

''Do you think he's prone to violence?''

Sawyer didn't think so, but he wasn't about to say anything until he knew what had happened. Bruce was his client; there were certain privileges to respect. ''Why do you ask?''

''I had conversations today with both his wife and his daughter. Apparently there was an ugly scene yesterday. Things were thrown around the room a little.''

''By my client?'' he asked, then saw no harm in rebutting it. ''That surprises me. To my knowledge, he's never been a violent man.''

''Are you sure?''

''I said 'to my knowledge.' Maybe the guy's been beating up women on the sly, but nothing's ever come out about it, and with a visible guy like Bruce, you'd think it would.''

"Nothing ever came out about the affair he was having."

"One woman. One affair. It had been going on for two or three months. No more."

That was the first Faith had heard of Bruce's side of the story, and while it was interesting, it wasn't surprising. Bruce's story was just that—Bruce's story. And it was Sawyer's job to relate it as told. "So he says."

"I believe him. And I do believe that he wouldn't hurt a woman. Unless those two are driving him mad."

"Sawyer..."

"They may be."

That wasn't Faith's immediate worry. "Beth was concerned for her mother's safety. I take it you don't think she has cause?"

"No, I don't."

"You sound sure."

"I feel sure."

"I'm glad one of us does. I'd feel horrible if I decided to let it go and then my client was batted around. But you say you know your client fairly well. I'm trusting you on this, Sawyer."

"I'm glad you can still trust me on something."

She was a minute in responding. "What do you mean?"

"After Friday night. I'm glad you still trust me a little."

"Of course, I trust you. I've always trusted you. Trust was never an issue."

But Sawyer saw it differently. "You trusted me to take care of you, and I didn't."

"Take care of me?"

"Protect you. I was thinking about this most of the day, and it's really bothering me. If you'd been with someone you trusted less on Friday night, you wouldn't have had half as much to drink. But you trusted me not to take advantage of you, so you may have been more lax than usual. Not only did I let us get carried away enough to make love, but I didn't think a thing about birth control. So now you're sitting there worrying that you're pregnant, because you have a successful career, and we all know that successful careers and babies don't mix."

Faith was astonished. "You spent most of today thinking about this?"

"While I was hammering away on the roof."

"I don't believe it, Sawyer." She took a breath. "Sawyer, do you know what year this is?"

"Of course I do."

"Then you'll know that these aren't the forties, or fifties, or even the seventies. Women have come a long way. Now, I know you don't like to think so— I know that, Sawyer, because much as I love you, you're a throwback to the heyday of male chauvinism. But really, we're not the pretty, dumb, helpless little things we used to be."

"I never said that, Faith—"

"But you imply it. I thought we agreed that on some level we both knew what we were doing Friday night. *You* were the one who said that first, and you're right. So I take at least half of the responsibility. And as far as a baby goes, I'm not sitting here worrying, because just as you said, there isn't a thing I can do until I know one way or the other, and even if I *am* pregnant, I have options! Honestly, Sawyer, these aren't the Dark Ages. I won't be sentenced to wear a scarlet letter on my breast. And I won't have to give up my practice. For your information, babies and careers are mixing better and better all the time." She stopped talking, but before he could say a word, she had another thought. This one riled her. "Ahhh. You're worried you'll have to marry me if I'm pregnant."

"That's not—"

"Save your breath, bud," she argued, suddenly and inexplicably furious. "I wasn't born yesterday, and that goes for experiencing marriage as well as understanding the male mind. I've been married once and it didn't work out. I'm not in a rush to go near it again, and I don't care if there *is* a baby involved. So you can sleep free of worry. No matter what happens, you won't be trapped." She slammed the receiver down hard.

Her hand was still pressing on the phone when it rang. White-knuckled, she picked it up. "Leave it, Sawyer. You've said enough for one night." She hung up again.

This time when the phone rang, she lifted the handset, but dropped it right back without even putting it to her ear. Before it could ring again, she took it off the hook.

Angrily she stalked across the living room, stood for a minute at the window with her arms pressed tightly across her breasts, then stalked back and headed for the bedroom. She wasn't quite sure what had gotten out of hand, but something had. All she'd done was to call him in concern over her client. It had been a professional call, that was all.

Storming back through the apartment, she put the phone back on its hook and dialed Sawyer's number. The instant she heard his gruff hello, she said in her most confident and business-like tone, "From what the Leindecker women have told me, we don't yet have grounds for a restraining order, but that may change. Please advise your client that if he continues to torment his wife, he'll give us those grounds." She hung up before Sawyer could get in a word.

Sawyer was livid. Sitting in the dark in his apartment that night, he couldn't remember ever being quite so angry with anyone as he was with Faith. He'd known she had an emotional bent, but he hadn't dreamed that she'd be so quick to fly off the handle at remarks as innocent as the ones he'd made.

Good Lord, she knew he was old-fashioned when it came to traditional male-female values. She'd told him so dozens of times. She'd *ribbed* him about it, which meant that she didn't think it was all bad. He certainly didn't. He liked to think he was honest and responsible. And chivalrous. Those were good things. They showed respect for a woman, and he certainly respected Faith. He might be furious with her, but he respected her—respected and trusted her, which was why he'd marry her in a minute if she was pregnant, and he'd do it happily. He wasn't committed to life as a single. Granted, it was nice to be free of Joanna's smothering, but freedom brought loneliness. Besides, Faith wasn't a smotherer.

God forbid!

She wasn't a smotherer, but she sure as hell was stubborn and hotheaded and...passionate. Ah, yes, she was that. Just as there had been fire in her voice tonight, there had been fire in her body Friday night. He couldn't forget it. His body wouldn't let him. Those same flashes of memory he'd seen through a haze on Saturday morning came to him now, only the haze had cleared.

He saw her as she'd come from the bedroom after she'd changed, wearing an over-size sweatshirt that hid her body, and slim jeans that didn't. He saw the way she'd smiled up at him, her sandy hair covering her forehead in bangs, framing her face in a gentle bob that ended an inch below her chin. He saw hazel eyes that weren't spectacular in and of themselves, but that reflected what was inside, in turn intelligence, mischief, curiosity, enthusiasm and desire. He saw a small, straight nose and lips that were as whimsical as her firm chin wasn't.

Then he saw her naked in the night light, a vision that made his body harden. Her breasts were full, larger than he'd thought, though perhaps firm was the word, he decided. Her waist was slim, her hips flaring just enough to brand her a woman in ways that boyishly slim models couldn't be branded. And inside—inside she was hot and moist, welcoming, generous and demanding.

He wanted her, and he wanted her badly. One night—half-zonked, but obviously not zonked enough—and he was in physical pain. Hadn't he ever seen it coming? Over and over he asked himself that question, but he wasn't able to come up with an answer. He'd known Faith for over ten years, yet things that seemed so clear to him now—such as her sex appeal and his response to it—simply hadn't occurred to him before. He'd viewed her as a friend, seeing only what was appropriate for a friend to see, overlooking the rest.

He couldn't see her that way anymore. That point of view had been lost beneath two bodies writhing on Faith's carpet Friday night. No longer could he view her only as a friend. After tonight, he wondered if she'd let him see her even as that. She was angry because she thought he was worried she'd hook him into marriage. Well, *he* was angry because she *thought* that! But she hadn't let him say a word, and that was the most infuriating part of it, as far as he was concerned. He didn't like being cut off. He didn't like being silenced when he had something to say. And he particularly didn't like being silenced by a woman.

That was why, shortly before ten the next morning, he barreled through the door of Faith's suite, tipped a finger from his forehead to Loni as he swept past, went into Faith's office and swung the door shut behind him.

She was on the phone, but the stormy look on his face wasn't to be ignored. Nor was the way he planted his hands apart on the outside edge of her desk and, leaning forward, waited. Speedily and with as much finesse as she could manage, she got off the phone. The instant the instrument was out of her hand, he opened fire.

"Don't ever do that to me again, Faith. I'm not a stupid man, and I don't say stupid things. If you have an accusation to make, make it and let me rebut it. That's the way things are done in this world. Nothing gets accomplished when a person makes an accusation and then turns and runs away."

"I didn't run away."

"Figuratively you did. You thought you knew what I was thinking and you didn't like it, so you flipped out, then you hung up on me—four times—without letting me explain myself. That was rude, Faith. *Rude.* What's the matter? Were you afraid to hear what I had to say?"

"Of course not."

"I think you were. I think you knew that I'd come out smelling like a rose, because I wasn't thinking about marriage or being trapped. I wasn't thinking about myself when I talked about the chance of a baby, only you. You're the one whose body would be affected, and you can argue until you're blue in the face, but that's a fact, Faith. As far as conception goes, my body does its thing in seconds, then it's done, while yours is just beginning, so you're the one who'll bear the brunt of a pregnancy.''

"I know the facts of life."

"I'm glad to hear that, because you obviously don't know the facts of friendship. A friend doesn't desert a friend when she's in trouble. Even if there wasn't the slightest chance that I was the one who got you into trouble, I'd still be concerned. Okay, so we share the blame for what happened. I'll buy that. But I still feel guilty. I still feel I should have been more responsible.'' He rushed on when she opened her mouth. "And it doesn't have a goddamned thing to do with selfishness. I was thinking of you. I still am. I'm concerned for you as a friend. And lover.''

"Sawyer—"

"I'm concerned, Faith. But you don't want to think that. You want to be angry with me.''

"Why would I want that?''

"So that you don't have to think of being attracted to me. You want to think of last Friday night as a mistake, because maybe you've thought about it a lot, and you're feeling things you don't want to.''

"Like attraction?'' She tried to make light of it. "You're a *friend*, Sawyer. You've said it a million times. We were tipsy.''

He leaned closer. His voice grew deeper, sounding alternately vehement and sensual. "We were aroused. We did it to each other, Faith. If you're honest with yourself, you'll admit that.''

"We were tipsy.''

Very slowly he straightened. The muscle in his jaw

flexed. His eyes never left her face as he came around the desk.

"What are you doing, Sawyer?"

"Making my point."

"What's that supposed to mean?" She tried to sound curious rather than nervous, still she backed up a little in her chair. He was very tall, dark and imposing in his navy suit with his eyes so intent.

"I think we have a problem. I think we stumbled onto something Friday night that's not going to go away."

"Look, Sawyer, if it's the thing about a baby that's got you worried—"

"I don't give a damn about that." He bent over, putting his hands on the arms of her chair. "It's the other."

"What other?"

"The attraction."

"There *isn't* any attraction. I *told* you." She flattened a hand on his shirt to hold him off. "Don't, Sawyer. This is very unprofessional. It's criminal. It's...assault."

His face hovered over hers. "No assault."

"Please," she begged, breathing shallowly. "Leave now. Loni's sitting right out there. If I have to scream—"

"No scream. You know damn well that I won't hurt you."

"I don't want this, Sawyer. I don't want this. Please. Sawyer, this isn't *you*—"

His mouth took hers, and she was right. There was

none of the teasing, none of the sampling, none of the gentleness he'd shown her on Friday night. His kiss contained the hunger that had been building since then, a hunger that he'd tried to ignore himself until he'd realized the futility of it.

Faith tried to turn her head, but he thrust a hand into her hair and held her still. When she tried to push him away, he took one of her hands, drew her right out of the chair and against him, where she was effectively immobilized. She even tried to keep her mouth closed and rigid, but she was no match for his persistence. The firm stroking of his lips was powerful; they kneaded the resistance from hers as though it had never been, then rewarded her pliancy with the kind of kiss she hadn't believed existed. It was wet and warm, unbelievably erotic. She was shaking inside, sagging weakly against him by the time he raised his head.

Unable to stand, she sank back into her chair. She knew Sawyer had allowed it, or he'd still have her clamped against him, but she wasn't about to thank him.

"Well?" he demanded. His voice was hoarse.

It was a minute before she could say anything. Then, eyes downcast, she whispered, "You've made your point."

"I didn't catch that."

"You caught it."

"Look at me and repeat it."

"What for? So your victory will be complete?"

He caught her chin and turned her face up. "No

victory. I'm feeling as frustrated now as you are, but you're right, I made my point."

"And you're happy?"

"Fat chance. I have to be in court at eleven, then again at two on separate cases. I've got clients coming in at four and five-thirty. I have to prepare a motion that's due tomorrow. Somewhere in the middle, I'll have to return half a dozen phone calls and call Bruce Leindecker to discuss the issue of violence. So I'm frustrated as hell, but I can't do a thing about it. Happy? Not by a long shot."

Turning, he thundered from her office with nearly the same air of belligerence that had carried him in in the first place.

Sawyer didn't like starting days off that way. When he did, they invariably went downhill, and this day was no exception. The court appearance at eleven was forfeited when his client didn't show, and the one at two resulted in a continuance. He couldn't get a bead on the motion he had to prepare, because the phone kept ringing even after he'd returned the obligatory calls. The client who came in at four reported that he had inadvertently destroyed a piece of exculpatory evidence, and the client who was scheduled for five-thirty called to say he'd be an hour late.

So Sawyer called Bruce Leindecker and received an earful the likes of which he wasn't prepared for.

"The woman's crazy," Bruce claimed in a voice that lacked its customary composure. "Something's happened to her. After being utterly stoic for twenty-four years, she's suddenly turned violent.''

''Violent?'' That was a new twist. ''Your wife?''

''Yes. I walked into the house on Saturday. I was prepared to sit down with her and try to explain why I did what I did, but she wouldn't listen. She kept cutting me off, telling me how cruel I am and how she's given me the best years of her life. I couldn't get a word in edgewise, but I kept trying, and that made her even more angry. So she started throwing things.''

Sawyer knew all too well about trying to get a word in edgewise. He also knew how successfully an irate woman could prevent it. He didn't know about throwing things, though. ''*She* was throwing things?''

''A cup and saucer that we'd bought in Ireland, a vase filled with flowers, the engraved picture frame that I'd given her for our twentieth anniversary. She went berserk!''

''Did she hit you?''

''No, but not for lack of trying. She's a lousy shot. Never could do anything athletic. She broke her arm when we were playing tennis in the Bahamas, fell off a donkey when we were touring the Grand Canyon, tripped and broke her ankle on the steps of the Louvre when we were in Paris. Athletic? Hah! She couldn't hit me with her eyes closed.''

Bruce's irritation was real, still Sawyer sensed a ghost of indulgence beneath it. ''But she kept trying?''

''Over and over, and our daughter stood there

cheering her on.'' The indulgence vanished. "Beth is ticked off at me because I wouldn't give her a job. Well, hell, she was in the bottom third of her graduating class, not because she didn't have the brains, but because she didn't want to study. Is this a good recommendation, I ask you? And did I treat her any different from her brother? No, sir. I wouldn't give him a job, either. It's unhealthy for children to train in their father's business. Far better that they train somewhere else then come back with fresh ideas. But she wanted the easy way out. She figured she could have her cake and eat it too—have a job like a career woman, but still be able to play like her mother does.''

Sawyer cleared his throat. "What does her mother—your wife—do, exactly?"

"Shop. Play cards. Meet friends for lunch.''

"Has she ever done any work for you?"

"In the early days she did some typing and filing, but once the business started to grow, she retired. She comes into the office once a year to do the Christmas party, which is just fine. She doesn't have a mind for business. She does throw a good party, though. She gets the best people and she makes sure that they don't rob us blind. Caterers do that, you know. Especially with corporate clients. Laura is wise to things like that.''

"It's a good quality for the wife of a man in your position.''

As though only then realizing what he'd said, Bruce compensated by turning gruff. "The wife of a man in my position should know not to make a scene in the office about his indiscretions. She should know not to run to a lawyer the first chance she gets. And she should know not to bar him from his own home. I put up with that for one night, but that was it. I have never been, nor am I now a violent man, but when my wife unfairly cuts me off, when she won't even let me explain myself, I refuse to sit idly by and take it.''

Sawyer could identify with that, too. Faith had frustrated him nearly beyond belief by repeatedly hanging up on him. The frustration had built and built through the night, so that by the time he'd stormed into her office that morning, he was harboring feelings that had bordered on the violent. "What, exactly, did you do?" he asked Bruce, as curious as he was wary.

"I lost my temper, knocked a few things on the floor, but they were harmless things," he added quickly, "like letters and magazines and folded laundry. She leaves the laundry on the stairs every day. It's the most annoying thing. She finally carries it up before she goes to bed, but in the meantime it sits there staring at me."

Sawyer wouldn't mind laundry staring at him as long as it was clean and had been made so by someone other than himself. Of all the chores he'd come into since his divorce, doing laundry was the worst. "Be grateful she does it for you."

"She doesn't. The laundress does. But the laundress doesn't go upstairs. Only the cleaning girl does that, and you can't expect the cleaning girl to be putting personal things away, Laura says. I suppose she has a point. My laundry is always clean when I need it, so I really can't complain.'' His voice hardened. ''I can complain about other things, though. The problem is that I haven't. I've kept my mouth shut too long. So now when I open it to her for the first time, she feels threatened. Well, she should!''

Sawyer would have raised an arm and shouted, ''Right on!'' if it hadn't been for the one point his client was conveniently forgetting. The marriage, for all its faults, had endured for twenty-four years until Bruce had cheated on his wife. Sawyer wasn't condemning him for it. That wasn't his job. His job was to best advise and represent Bruce in any divorce action that might be taken, and since misbehavior now could become a factor later, caution seemed the way to go.

''What I want you to do,'' he said, ''is to cool it a little. If she's threatened because you're speaking up to her at home for the first time, that's one thing. But if the threat becomes physical, or she *perceives* it as being physical, that's another.''

Bruce was indignant. ''I wouldn't touch her. I'm not that kind of man.''

''I know, but sometimes when men are provoked they do things they wouldn't normally do. It sounds to me like your wife is provoking you these days.''

''That's an understatement.''

''It also sounds like you've got a real communication problem.''

''Maybe,'' Bruce admitted.

"Are you determined to stay at the house?"

"Yes. At least until she listens to my side of the story."

Sawyer paused, then asked slowly, "Do you want this divorce?" As things stood the Friday before when they'd last spoken, Bruce had been ready to file papers. He'd been angry, of course, mostly at the way his wife had confronted him, and he'd been frightened by Laura's hiring Faith, which was why he'd been so quick to put Sawyer on retainer. Apparently either the anger and fear had faded, or simply shifted in focus.

Good businessman that he was, Bruce said, "I'm making no decisions yet."

"Do you think you can salvage the marriage?"

"I don't know. She's furious. I've never seen her furious before."

"You've never cheated on her before. That does something to a woman."

"I suppose."

"Look, I'm not making judgments. I don't pretend to know what your marriage was like or what caused the affair at the Four Seasons. You should know, though, and if you don't, you'd better try to find out. Communication is the key. I can mediate things, but only to a point. Have you considered going to a counselor?"

"I haven't had time to consider much of anything. I'm too busy trying to make sure she doesn't have the locks on the house changed while I'm at work."

"Would she do that?"

"If she does, I'll put a stop on her charge cards."

"Did you tell her that?"

"Yes, sir."

"Have you told her you're not sure you want a divorce?"

"I told her I'd fight her. I didn't say whether I was talking about the divorce itself or a settlement. I just wanted her to know that I won't be a pansy anymore when it comes to her. If she wants to fight, I'll show her how it's done."

"Be cautious. I can't advise that enough. Be cautious." He hesitated. "One last thought. The affair— is it really over?"

"It's over."

"So if your wife were to hire a private investigator, he wouldn't find you anywhere you shouldn't be?"

"No, sir."

"That's good. There's no need to rile her up any more than she already is. Legally you have every right to stay at the house, but while you're doing it, try to give her some breathing space. Let her calm down a little. Maybe then you'll be able to talk."

Long after Sawyer hung up the phone he thought about that advice. It applied to Faith and him, he knew. Their relationship had taken several dramatic twists in less than three days, and in the process emotions had been stirred. Those emotions had to simmer a bit, then settle. Maybe, he mused, he and Faith would be best not seeing each other for a few days.

It was an ironic thought. He hadn't seen Faith for *weeks* before last Friday. Their paths just hadn't crossed often lately. Yet they were best of friends. When they were together, they picked up right where they had left off. They were thoroughly compatible.

They'd always been so. He thought back to the times they'd spent together during law school, where they'd met, and then after, when they'd been establishing themselves in the legal world. They'd always been close, regardless of how frequently or infrequently they saw each other. There was one big difference between those earlier times and now, of course. They'd felt safe then, unthreatened by each other because they were married to other people.

Now they were free, which was certainly why they'd allowed Friday night to happen. But he wasn't sorry it had. He'd done his share of socializing since he and Joanna were divorced, and Faith was head and shoulders above those other women. Sure, it had been a shock waking up in her bed. It had been a shock realizing the way their making love had happened. And it was going to necessitate a rethinking of their relationship. But he wasn't convinced their becoming more than friends was so terrible.

The problem was to convince Faith of that.

6

Faith spent the week trying to convince herself that Sawyer was nothing but a good friend, a fellow lawyer with whom she just happened to share a case, and a one-time lover. The last caused her the most problem, because much as she tried she couldn't forget the way he'd kissed her. Not when he was making love to her on the rug in the urban nightlight. But when he'd kissed her in her office in the bold light of morning.

He hadn't been drunk then, not even tipsy. There had been nothing to blur his judgment, still he'd kissed her like a lover, and she'd responded. Worse, the response hadn't ended when he'd walked out the door. It had burrowed deep inside, making her restless ever since.

He'd made his point, all right. She was attracted to him—which was just fine, she told herself. Just because a woman was attracted to a man didn't mean there had to be a heavy relationship. She didn't want a heavy relationship. She'd been through the disillusionment of one that had petered out, scattering hopes and dreams to the wind. Now she was enjoying her freedom, and if there were times when she thought of such things as having a family, she reminded herself that she had time. She was only thirty-three. Not over the hill quite yet.

Still her thoughts kept returning to Sawyer and that kiss. It had been, without a doubt, the most exciting kiss she'd ever received. As conservative as he looked on the outside, that kiss had been wild and unconstrained, and he hadn't apologized for it—not when he'd given it, nor in the hours after.

Hours stretched into days, and she didn't hear from him. She was alert when she passed through the lobby of the office building they shared, when she walked through the nearby streets, even when she was in the courthouse, but she didn't catch sight of him once.

Finally Friday morning, she had what she felt was a legitimate reason to call. She reached him at the office on the second try, just as he returned from an appointment.

"Hi, Sawyer." She sounded calm, despite the acceleration of her pulse. She wasn't sure how she'd be received.

"Faith!" He shrugged out of his trenchcoat, only mildly winded from the dash through the rain and up the stairs. "I just got in."

"I'm sorry to bother you."

"No bother." He was inordinately pleased that she'd called, inordinately pleased that she sounded amiable, given the way they'd last parted. "Is everything okay?"

On one hand, it was. His tone of voice, enthusiastic but with that last bit of concern, was the Sawyer she knew and loved. She felt back on stable ground, at least where he was concerned.

On the other hand, there was no stable ground at her client's house. "Laura Leindecker just called. Her husband's gone. After sticking to her like glue all week, he just…disappeared. You haven't by chance heard from him, have you?"

Sawyer frowned. "Not since Monday. When was the last time she saw him?"

"Yesterday morning. He didn't come back to the house last night."

"I'd have thought she'd be pleased. She wanted him out."

"She's worried. It may be habit, still she's worried."

Tossing his trenchcoat aside, he dropped into his chair. "Are you sure the word isn't suspicious?" he asked, but in a curious way, rather than a snide one. "Maybe she's thinking he's with another woman."

Faith had wondered about that, had even dared ask it. Laura had been uneasy with the question. "It would be impossible for her not to be suspicious. She found that note. He admitted to being unfaithful. A basic trust was destroyed then." She paused, trying to hone in on her instincts and convey them to one who might help. "Laura wants to be able to say that he's with another woman, but I think her worry goes deeper. I think she's genuinely concerned."

"Has she called the office?"

"She was embarrassed to do it herself, so she had

her cleaning girl do it. He wasn't there. His secretary said he was out for the day.''

''Maybe he's away on business.''

''He didn't pack any things. I thought maybe he'd contacted you, but if he hasn't—''

''Let me make a few calls.'' Sawyer had already flipped through the pink slips that were sitting on his desk. None had to do with Bruce Leindecker. ''I may be able to push the right buttons and get some information. Will you be in the office for a little while?''

''I won't go anywhere until you call back. Thanks, Sawyer.''

As she quietly hung up the phone, she realized that she felt better than she had all week. She liked having Sawyer on her side. He'd been there for so many years, an able resource person, a shoulder to lean on. Strange that their doing something as intimate as making love should pit them against each other—and it had done that, more so than the Leindecker case. If she was lucky, maybe the Leindecker case would be the thing to get them back on the track of being friends. He had certainly been the old, dependable, agreeable, helpful Sawyer a minute ago.

He was all of those things when he called back half an hour later. ''Bruce is fine. He's with their son, Tim, in Longmeadow.''

Faith let out a soft breath. ''Laura will be relieved. She'll also be furious. Why didn't he tell her where he was going?''

''He didn't know where he was going until he got

there. He's pretty upset about all this. Wasn't sure Laura would give a damn.''

"Of course, she gives a damn. They've been married for twenty-four years.''

"Apparently she's been cursing that fact in no un-certain terms all week.''

"He's been in her hair all week.''

"So he figured he'd give her a break. He needed one, too.''

"Maybe Tim will be a calming force.''

Sawyer would have liked that, but the brief time he'd spent talking with Tim on the phone wasn't re-assuring. ''I...wouldn't count on it.''

"Uh-oh,'' Faith said. "What's Tim's gripe?''

"He got married last year. Laura doesn't like his wife. Doesn't think she's good enough. There are some hard feelings, I guess.''

"You guess,'' Faith murmured. The Leindecker case, like many of the other divorces she'd handled, was beginning to sound like a soap opera. But she was being paid to consider each new plot twist. "I guess I'd better call Laura and tell her Bruce is all right. Did he say when he'll be home?''

"When I asked, he got a little annoyed. He said that he's too old to be reporting in, and anyway, she kicked him out, he says. I told him to remember that she was worried. Maybe you could tell her to bear with him.''

"I think I can do that,'' Faith said and reflected on the discussion. Laura swore that she wanted a divorce, which was why Faith had accepted a retainer. But there were times when Faith wondered. "Are we negotiating a divorce here, or mediating a marital squabble? I mean, I'm all for encouraging reconciliation, but I'm a lawyer, not a therapist."

"Mmm. It gets tedious sometimes."

"Do you ever want out?" she asked, thinking in broader terms.

"Lots of times. That's why divorce work is only a small part of my practice. What about you? You do it more often than me."

"I don't like the tedium either. But there's probably less of it in the cases I do. Mostly I represent women, and women are the underdogs in most divorce proceedings nowadays."

"Is Laura Leindecker an underdog?"

"I'm...not quite sure. I'm not quite sure about lots of things relating to this case."

"Ditto," Sawyer said, but he was more interested in other things about which he wasn't quite sure. "I'm heading down to the Cape first thing in the morning. Want to come?"

It was a minute before Faith adjusted to the shift in gears, and even then, the invitation had popped out so suddenly that she couldn't take it seriously. "Uh, thanks, Sawyer, but I've got a million things to do tomorrow."

"Do them today."

"I'm working today."

"Tonight. Do your million things tonight. Come with me tomorrow." His voice was deep and earnest.

"You're serious," she said, realizing it just then.

"Of course, I'm serious. Did you doubt it?"

"I...yes. It seemed like such an unpremeditated suggestion."

"It was, but it's a good one. I want you to see the house."

Faith wanted to see it, too. She also wanted to spend time with Sawyer, who was nicer to be with than just about anyone she knew. She'd have agreed to go in a minute—if it hadn't been for the Friday night before. Thanks to that night, something more than friendship existed between them. She'd spent far too much time thinking about that something than she cared to admit. It had haunted her—the flash of his large hand molding her breast, the wetness of his mouth on her belly, the piercing strength of him as he filled her from the inside out. The haunting made her weak in the knees, and weak in the knees translated into weak in resolve, and without resolve, she didn't trust herself.

"I don't know, Sawyer," she said so softly that her message came across loud and clear.

"Nothing has to happen," he assured her in a voice that was every bit as quiet, but far more sure. "There's nothing remotely seductive or romantic about the place. It's old and broken-down. I'm re-shingling the roof. I work the whole time I'm there, and when I'm done working, I'm tired."

He was trying to paint an unappealing picture, she knew, but he failed. The image of Sawyer Bell on the roof doing physical labor was enticing. "So if you're working all the time, what will I do?"

"Look around and decide whether you think I ought to torch the place."

"You can't torch it, Sawyer. Besides, my looking around won't take long. What do I do when I'm done with that?"

"Strip paint from the moldings around the fireplace."

"You'd put me to work?"

"If you're bored. It's good therapy. We agreed on that, remember?"

She remembered, but that didn't alter the fact that if she went to the Cape with him, they'd be together for an extended period of time. A body could only work so long. When it was done working, it could get into mischief.

"I don't know," she said again. This time her voice was softened by a blend of wistfulness and apprehension. "You'll want to stay overnight."

Sawyer hesitated for just a minute. "Yes." He knew what she was thinking. "Nothing has to happen, Faith. We can spend the day working, then go out to dinner and catch a movie or something."

"Where would we sleep?"

"Wherever you want."

"Where do you usually sleep?"

"In a sleeping bag on the floor. But that doesn't mean you have to do it. The floor is warped. It's worse than sleeping on bare ground. It's fine for me, but I wouldn't expect you to rough it that way."

"I'm not fragile."

"You're used to comfort."

"That doesn't mean I can't live without it for a night. I'm not made of fluff."

"But you're a woman."

"So?"

"So your body doesn't conform as well to the floor as mine does. You have curves, Faith. My body is straighter and harder than yours."

For the space of a breath, Faith didn't speak. Then she murmured, "That's what worries me," and it was Sawyer's turn to be silent.

Finally he said quietly, "I want to be with you this weekend, and it doesn't have to be a sexual thing. It can be purely platonic. We'll be friends like we've always been. We won't do anything you don't want to do."

"That's what worries me," she repeated, and Sawyer understood.

"You don't trust yourself?" He hoped it was true. It wasn't that he was a sadist, just that he'd been aroused and aching too often that week. He wanted to think Faith had been, too.

"I'm not sure. I keep thinking about last Friday night and asking why I didn't stop what was happening. I guess—" she rushed on before he could remind her of the wine they'd drunk "—I'm not convinced I was out of it. I remember too many things too clearly."

Sawyer had been asking himself similar questions all week, but he wasn't about to discuss them now. If he could get Faith away with him, they'd have plenty of time to talk. "We won't have anything to drink this weekend. Nothing but coffee. Come with me, Faith. It'll be good for both of us."

"I don't want to make love."

"Then we won't."

"What if I ask for it?"

"Then we will."

"But I don't want to." She straightened in her chair. "Okay, Sawyer, I'll go down to the Cape with you on one condition. You have to keep things under control. I'm telling you now that I don't want to make love. It's your responsibility to make sure we don't, regardless of what I say when we're down there."

"That's absurd."

"I won't be able to relax with you unless you agree."

Sawyer brushed at the moisture breaking out over his lip. "That's just as absurd as the other. What if you find that you do want it? What if you're relaxed but making love will relax you even more? What if the pain of *not* making love is driving you crazy? What if you're begging me for it? Christ, Faith, I'm not a saint!"

"Then I won't go."

"I'll be a saint."

She had to smile at the speed of his turnaround. But before she could comment on it, he grumbled, "I wonder if this is what Leindecker's been going through all these years. A man thinks he's in control, then a woman gives him an ultimatum and he crumbles."

"Don't crumble. I'm counting on you to be strong.

That's your forte, Sawyer. You're a big, strong male. Much stronger than me—isn't that how the chauvinist credo reads?''

"Cute, Faith."

"But I'm serious, at least about your being strong. You are, and I'm trusting you." She paused. "Do you still want to go, or is the invitation rescinded?''

"We're going," he grumbled. "I'll pick you up at six tomorrow morning."

"*Six.* You didn't say anything about—''

"Six. Be ready, or I'm leaving without you."

Before Faith could argue, she was staring at the phone, which was dead in her hand. Replacing it in its cradle, she sat back in her chair, linked her fingers, pressed them to her mouth and wondered whether she was making a mistake. She'd given in to temptation, and though Sawyer had promised to save her from it—and though she trusted him to do just that—there was more to temptation than just sex.

Being with Sawyer, spending the entire weekend with him was a treat she couldn't pass up. She didn't have anything pressing to do over the weekend, and even if she had she couldn't think of anything that would appeal to her more than being with him.

Besides, she needed a weekend away.

Besides, she wouldn't mind stripping the moldings by the fireplace.

Besides, she liked the spontaneity of the whole thing.

So she was going. Feeling slightly scattered, even a little light-headed, she dropped her hands from her mouth and looked down to her desk to see what she had to do before she went home. It was a minute before she could make any sense of the papers strewn before her. They were the rough notes for a talk on family law she was delivering to a law school class the following Wednesday night, and she wanted it to be good. She wanted to teach her own full-term course one day; for that reason alone she had to impress both her students and whatever faculty members might be listening in.

But she wasn't in the mood for concentration just then, so she gathered the papers up, thinking to work on them at home that night. Taking a file from her cabinet, she set it with the papers, then, wiping her palms on her skirt, looked around the office for anything else she'd need.

Almost absently, she glanced at her watch and realized that it was only three o'clock. She couldn't leave for the day. Loni hadn't left. It was far too early—unless she had a court appearance or some other kind of appointment, which she didn't. So she sat back down in her chair and reached for the papers she'd so neatly piled together. She opened to the page she'd been reading, but ten minutes of staring at it without comprehending a word convinced her that it was best saved for another time.

Straightening the papers again, she slid them into her briefcase. Then she sat back, crossed her legs, took a pad of paper onto her lap and began to make a list of calls she wanted to make on Monday in reference to a client whose custody hearing was approaching. She had four names and numbers listed when, with a start, she realized that she hadn't called Laura Leindecker back.

Cursing her distraction, she immediately phoned the woman and passed on the information Sawyer had given her. Laura was relieved, then annoyed.

"Where does that leave me?" she asked. "Am I supposed to sit around all weekend and wait for him to come home?"

"What would you normally do?"

"Sit around all weekend and wait for him to come home. But I'm tired of doing that."

"Where will you go?"

"Out."

"What will you do?"

"Shop."

"Oh. Okay." Faith took a breath. "May I make a suggestion?"

"Please do."

"I think that perhaps you should start thinking about what you want from this divorce in terms of the division of property. Once we formally file papers, we'll get into those kinds of negotiations. It would help if you think about them now."

It was a new tack. Until then, Faith had focused on whether or not Laura wanted the divorce. From the start, Laura had insisted that she did, still Faith knew that the decision had been ruled by anger and hurt, far more than reason. Faith suspected that once Laura turned her thoughts to the specifics of getting divorced and *being* divorced, she might decide it wasn't what she wanted at all.

"I'll think about it," Laura said, but a bit defensively. "He'll fight me. He said he would."

"He doesn't want the divorce?"

"He *must* want it. After all, he's the one who found me so inadequate that he had to go looking for satisfaction with another woman."

Hearing Laura's hurt so bluntly expressed, Faith hurt for her in turn. "Have you asked him why he did that?" she asked gently.

Laura answered in an uneasy tone. "Went to another woman? I think it's obvious."

"Not necessarily. There are reasons why men do things, and being women, we don't always understand. It helps to ask sometimes."

"I can't. It would be too humiliating."

"It may not be as humiliating as you think. It may be that what your husband did had to do with him and something he's going through right now. It may have had little to do with you." She paused. When Laura didn't argue, she said, "Talk with him—if not about the affair, then about the divorce. And remember, stay calm. The calmer you are, the more you'll get from him. If he's determined to fight you, that's something we'll just have to face, but for now, the calmer you are, the better."

Stay calm. Stay clam. Those words became a litany in Faith's mind through the rest of that day. Each time she thought of going away with Sawyer, her stomach started to jump. She wasn't sure if it was excitement or nervousness, and she didn't stop to analyze which. She simply repeated the litany in her mind and went about doing everything she had to do to free herself up for Saturday and Sunday.

Actually, if it hadn't been for that jumping stomach, she'd never have made it out of bed when her alarm rang at five-thirty Saturday morning. She hadn't been able to fall asleep until after one, which meant that she was sleeping soundly when the alarm went off. It was pitch-black outside, still night in her book, but the instant she realized why she was getting up so early, her body came to life.

Quickly she showered, dried her hair and applied the lightest possible sheen of makeup. After pulling on a pair of jeans and a comfortable sweater, she put a change of clothes into an overnight bag, along with whatever else she decided she'd need for a rustic sleepover. She was zipping the bag when the doorbell rang.

Sawyer looked stern, dark and tired. She was certain something awful had happened to him, but when she asked, he merely shrugged. "I couldn't sleep." He straightened from the doorjamb which had been bearing the brunt of his weight. "Actually that's a lie. I purposely kept myself awake most of the night so that I'd be too tired to do anything tonight."

Faith closed her eyes to his self-mocking look. "Oh, Sawyer."

"You said it was my responsibility, so I'm making good on it." He reached for her bag. "Is this it?"

"We're only going overnight."

"But overnight usually means three changes of clothes, two jackets, boots, sneakers and flats, a makeup case, a hair dryer, a curling iron, a vacuum cleaner—"

Faith swept past him into the hall, tugged him out by the arm and slammed the door. She didn't say another word until he'd tucked her into the passenger's seat of his racy black Porsche. "Some car," she breathed, running a hand lightly over the butter-soft leather covering the seat. "Is it new?"

Sawyer took a deep breath. He knew he was being a pill, but he couldn't seem to help himself. He'd stayed up most of the night thinking of Faith, so not only was he tired, but his body was tight. It hadn't helped that he'd slept through his alarm. He'd had time for nothing but a record-fast shower. What he needed was coffee and fresh air.

"I got it six months ago," he said as he rolled down his window. "Usually I rent a pickup when I drive to the Cape. I need the space in back for tools and stuff."

"Why didn't you this time?"

"I wanted to impress you with the Porsche."

Studying his profile, she saw that he wasn't joking. She didn't know whether to yell at him or be pleased. In lieu of either, she said, "I'm impressed. But what are you going to do when you need the space for tools and stuff?"

"I won't this trip. Everything I need is already at the house." He shot her a quick glance, the first softened one since he'd arrived. "Did you have any trouble getting up?"

His glance warmed her. Still, she wasn't about to say that she'd jumped right out of bed in anticipation of seeing him, so she shrugged. "It'd be nice if the sun came up."

"It's coming," he said, and once they cruised their way free of the city buildings, she could see that it was. A faint strip of lavender lay on the eastern horizon with promise of daylight. She found that reassuring. When things were dark, the confines of the car were more intimate, and intimacy wasn't something she wanted to encourage.

They headed south on the expressway. Not long after they'd left the city, Sawyer took a short exit and pulled in at a coffee shop. "Black with one sugar?"

"Good memory."

"I'll be back."

Several minutes later he returned with two large coffees, a bag of donuts and more napkins than they'd use in a year. "Are you stocking up for the house?" she teased.

Sawyer didn't answer until he'd taken several healthy swallows of coffee. The fresh air had helped when it came to mellowing his mood; he was relying on caffeine to do the rest. "They're for the car. If something spills, I want to be able to clean it up."

Faith knew how things were between a man and his car. "Ahhh," she breathed in understanding, then pulled a honey-dipped donut from the bag and took a bite.

Sawyer demolished three in the time it took her to eat one. "I'm getting a refill of coffee. Want one?"

"No, thanks. This is fine."

He left the car, returned with a fresh cup of coffee, tore the cover enough to allow him to drink, then started the engine and returned to the road.

"How long will it take to get there?" she asked.

"An hour and a half. There won't be any traffic this time of day."

"I wonder why not," she murmured, but teasingly. With donuts filling her stomach and the warm smell of coffee filling the car, she was beginning to relax. Sawyer was a good driver. The car was a beauty. The dawning day was clear and bright. At that moment she was very glad she'd come.

The feeling was every bit as strong when Sawyer finally turned the Porsche off the main road onto the private one that wove through his property. Framed on either side by broad-leaved trees and shrubs, it narrowed, turned from hardtop to gravel and grew bumpy. He swore and slowed the Porsche to a crawl.

"Don't worry about me," Faith said, trying not to smile as she looked at him. "I don't mind the bumps." When he didn't answer, she gave in and laughed.

"What's so funny?"

"You. You look like you're in agony."

"I am."

"You're worried about the car. Don't be, Sawyer. It'll survive. What are shock absorbers for, anyway?"

Returning her gaze to the front window, she couldn't contain her surprise. "Sawyer?"

He was pulling up at a most unusual structure. Turning off the engine, he curved both hands over the top of the steering wheel. "This is it."

She let out her breath in a thoroughly confused, "Ahhh."

"What do you think?"

"I think...that you're right. The setting is great. The land is gorgeous, lush even this late in the season. Are those apple trees over there? But where's the lake? You said you were on a lake." She opened the door of the car and climbed out. "Is it behind the...house?" She took off in that direction, but she hadn't gone more than three steps into the soft grass when Sawyer caught her hand.

"You don't like it," he said.

"I think it's great."

"I'm not talking about the land. We both know that's great. But what about the house?"

She forced herself to focus on the building. It was tall, round and covered with aged bricks. "It looks like a water tower."

"That's what it is."

"But you called it a house."

"If a house is defined as a place to live in, this is a house. Come on. I want you to see the inside."

Faith allowed herself to be led to a doorway that looked as though it might crumble on the spot. The doorjamb was rotted and hanging off on one side. It was a miracle that the door stayed shut.

Not only did it stay shut, but it wouldn't open—at least, not until Sawyer pushed hard.

Inside, all was dark. Sawyer seemed to know what was where, though, because within seconds he produced a hurricane lamp and lit it. Holding it aloft, he guided her into the center of the room.

Cautiously, staying close enough to him to feel the reassuring warmth of his body, Faith looked around. The room was larger than she'd expected and empty save for Sawyer's roofing material piled to one side and a network of pipes that snaked up its walls. Those walls were of the same exposed brick as the exterior, and looked nearly as weathered. The floor was concrete, dirty and cracked. There wasn't a window in sight.

"This place is spooky," she whispered.

"But it has promise." Still holding her hand, he led her forward.

They were nearly on top of the far wall before she made out a door. Pushing it open, Sawyer led her into an annex that she hadn't been able to see from outside. It was rectangular, narrower than the water tower but deeper, and had windows, wallpapered walls, planked floors and a fireplace.

While it wasn't Versailles, it was a decided improvement on the water tower. She let out a breath. "Better. Much better."

Extinguishing the hurricane lamp, Sawyer set it aside. He took a long tube from the painted mantel above the fireplace, tipped out its contents and unrolled what were clearly an architect's plans for the renovation of the place. Spreading the plans on the floor, he began to explain them to her.

By the time he was done, Faith was sitting cross-legged beside him feeling the fool for her shortsightedness. "You're right," she admitted. "It does have promise. Once windows are cut in the water tower and a sleeping loft is built above the living room, it'll be completely different."

Sawyer looked around the annex. "Once the door is widened and this place is gutted and rebuilt with modern kitchen and bathing facilities, it'll be even *more* different. I agree, it's pretty depressing right now. But there was something about it that appealed to me right away—maybe its isolation, or the woods or the lake, or the uniqueness of the whole thing. I guess that was it. The uniqueness." He gave Faith a smile that melted whatever chill may have seeped into her from the innards of the tower. "Who else do you know who can say that he lives in a converted water tower?"

"Not a soul." She looked back at the plans and grinned. "Not a soul. Unique is the word, all right."

"So you think I should go ahead with it?"

Her grin lingered when she raised her eyes to his. "Definitely. I think it's a super project."

"Don't think I should torch it?"

"You can't. Brick won't burn."

Other things could, though, and Faith suddenly grew aware of them—Sawyer's brown eyes darker than they'd been but warmer, heating her cheeks, her mind, her blood. She could do without that kind of burning, too.

Scrambling to her feet, she brushed off the seat of her pants. "Are we working?"

"We're working."

"Let's get to it, then. From the looks of those plans, there's plenty to do."

7

Sawyer didn't plan to do all the work himself. He would have liked to, but he knew his limitations. For starters, time was a factor. At the rate of two weekends a month, it would take him years to make the place livable. He wanted to be able to enjoy it before that. And then there was the matter of skill. He was a lawyer, not a carpenter or a mason or a millworker. He knew how to reshingle a roof, how to refinish floors, how to miter moldings, even how to install cabinets, but when it came to carving windows through brick, wiring an electrical system, designing a heating system and installing new plumbing, he was willing to yield to the experts.

He told Faith as much when they took a break for lunch, which consisted of burgers at a diner on the way into town. "There's no point in doing it if it isn't done right. I don't want to end up with something that will blow apart when the first coastal storm hits."

Faith had spent a good part of the morning in and out of the water tower, first relaying shingles up to Sawyer, then trying to familiarize herself with the tower so she wouldn't shiver each time she walked in. Putting a jacket over her sweater helped beat the chill; she wasn't quite as successful fighting the heeby-jeebies.

"That water tower would withstand an assault by Attila the Hun," she maintained in a wry tone of voice.

Sawyer grinned. "Solid, huh?"

His grin was filled with pride, but it wasn't pride that suffused Faith's insides with a now familiar heat. It was the grin itself, a slash of lips and teeth that was a little curious, a little daring, a little wicked and very, very masculine. And the grin came often. With the drive behind them, with Sawyer fully awake, with the worst of his frustration expended on the roof, he was in the best of moods.

As far as Faith was concerned, that was dangerous. Each time he grinned, she felt tiny prickles of awareness march through her belly. She tried to think back to the days when he grinned and she enjoyed it in an innocent way, but those days seemed an eon ago. She wasn't sure she was ever again going to be able to see Sawyer's grin without melting a little inside.

The water tower, she supposed, was in apt counterpoint to what she was feeling. "Very solid," she confirmed.

His grin relaxed when he took a large bite of his sandwich, but all that did was to shift her awareness from his mouth to his other features. Though he'd washed up before they left the house, he still had the rugged look of a workman. Part of it was due, she was sure, to the gray athletic T-shirt he wore under a faded flannel shirt, jeans that were old, worn and thin, and work boots. The other part was due to the muss of his dark hair, the ruddy color on his cheeks, the size and sinewed strength of his hands, and the power of his features, which seemed, here in the country, more exposed than usual.

Faith needed a diversion. "How did you find the tower? Had you been looking for land down here?"

"Not exactly," he said, but he, too, was distracted. The look in her eyes just then had been full of the kind of appreciation that men dreamed of receiving from lovely women. She fought it; he could see how she deliberately brought herself back, but for several minutes she'd been swept up by something over which she had little control.

That was a good sign, he decided. Faith had a thing about control. She was a harsh taskmaster when it came to ruling herself. It would do her good to lose control once in a while.

As long as he didn't. He'd promised her.

Clearing his throat, he finished his burger off in a bite. When it had gone the way of both its predecessor and a large order of fries, he said, "I got lost, actually. I was visiting friends who were renting a place down here, and I got the directions screwed up. I wound up at the water tower, and it intrigued me."

"Did you know it was for sale?"

"Not then. I finally managed to get where I was supposed to go, and I went back to Boston at the end of the day, but I kept thinking about the tower. It looked abandoned. So I made a few calls, found out that the whole parcel of land was for sale and came down the next weekend to look again."

Faith remembered some of the discussions she'd had with Sawyer way back when. "You always wanted a vacation place. You used to talk about finding something in northern Maine."

"Mmm. Joanna hated that idea. She may have been as maternal as they came, but Earth Mother she wasn't. The thought of being too far from civilization frightened her."

"She'd have liked it down here. You're isolated, but you're not."

"Her loss."

"Your gain. It's really a super place, Sawyer."

He raised two fingers to the waitress and called for coffee. "It'll be even more super when it's done. It won't ever be big, but the way the architect has it planned, there'll be room for everything I want. It'll be a year-round escape." Putting his weight on his elbows, he met her gaze with a look that was frank and unguarded. "I've wanted something like this for years. I wanted it when I was a kid, only my parents couldn't afford their own house, let alone a vacation place. I wanted it when Joanna and I first married, only I didn't have the money then, either. Joanna was the one who bought the house in Cambridge. I was getting benefits from Uncle Sam, and that helped a lot when I was in school, but even when I finally graduated, it was a while before I hit the upper brackets."

The waitress came with their coffee. Sawyer

handed Faith a packet of sugar, took two for himself and two thimbles of cream, and focused on the mocha-colored brew as he stirred it. "By the time I had enough in the bank to think about a second home, Joanna and I were on the skids. I felt badly about that. She deserved more of the fruits of her labor than she got. I didn't take care of her very well, at least not during our marriage."

Faith had to smile, but it was a smile made soft by understanding and admiration. Sawyer was, indeed, a throwback to the days where men took care of women. She didn't find it offensive just then, though. As he talked so quietly and honestly, she saw him for the protective and caring man that he was. Joanna, with her need to protect rather than be protected, to care for rather than be cared for, couldn't appreciate him.

Faith could. The thought surprised her, because she saw herself as a thoroughly independent woman, but at that moment, away from the city and her thoroughly independent world, she found the idea of being protected and cared for strangely appealing.

"Does Joanna know what she gave up?" she heard herself ask.

If there was a compliment inherent in the question, Sawyer missed it. He was shifting his coffee cup in its saucer, studying each turn. "She didn't give up so much. When I was in school, I studied most of the time. When I got a job, I worked most of the time. I wasn't much of a companion for her. I think she was as relieved as I was when we finally called it quits."

"Who handled the divorce?"

"Me. It was an easy thing. We agreed on the property settlement. I gave most everything and then some. She'd earned it."

"You are a good man."

He looked up at her. "I like to think I'm a fair one. The marriage wasn't going anywhere, but Joanna had invested a great deal of time and effort in me. Largely thanks to her, I was healthy and productive. She deserved a good settlement. I wasn't about to rob her of it just because I knew I could get away with it in court." He paused, frowned. "Why is it we always end up talking about the past?"

"Because it's part of us. You went through a lot with Joanna. Just because the marriage is over doesn't mean you forget her."

"Is it the same with you and Jack?"

"I don't know," Faith said. She shifted her gaze to the counter, but she was oblivious to the people perched on leather-covered stools at the bar. "Jack and I didn't go through anything like you and Joanna did. He was just there. I went about my life, he went about his. It was an increasingly uninteresting relationship."

"Was it interesting when you first met him?"

Sitting back in the booth, she looked down at her hands. "I'm not sure."

"Did you love him?"

"I guess so."

"You weren't sure?"

Faith raised her head and spoke in her own defense.

"I had to do something. I was fresh out of college, just starting law school, and it seemed that everywhere I turned, someone was telling me that if I didn't marry soon, I never would. They said that once I became a career woman I wouldn't have time for anything else. They said that if I was successful, I'd become so threatening to men that none of them would come close." Her words stopped. She shrugged. The ghost of a smile touched her lips and was gone. "I guess I bought it all."

"Who was doing the selling?"

She didn't answer at first. Disloyalty wasn't something she took pride in, and this time there was no wine to blunt the effect. But Sawyer was waiting for an honest answer—Sawyer, whom she trusted. "My family."

Studying her face, he saw a vulnerability that was entirely new. Gently he said, "I've never heard you talk about your family before."

"I try not to."

"You don't get along?"

"Oh, we get along just fine, as long as we don't discuss anything more weighty than the price of eggs."

"They don't live nearby, do they?" He was sure he'd have known if they did, principally because Faith would have been more involved with them.

"They're in Oregon."

"And you're on the opposite coast. By design?"

She pursed her lips, thought for a minute, gave a single slow nod.

"Safer that way?"

"You got it. My parents are very conventional people, and I'm not criticizing that. But I'm not conventional by their standards, and they do criticize me. I go back to visit once a year. That's enough."

"They must be proud of your work."

"They know nothing about it, other than that I'm a lawyer. For all of their interest in that, I could be a toll collector on the turnpike. I've tried to tell them about what I do. I've described some of the more interesting cases I've handled, but as soon as I stop for a breath, they're asking me whether or not I'm dating."

"Did they like Jack?"

"Jack was a husband. That pleased them. But then the questions started coming about babies, and when I told them I wasn't ready to have kids, that set them off. They always found something cutting to say. I've never fit into the mold of what they think a woman should be." Faith chewed on the inside of her lip for a minute. Slowly she released it and in a small voice said, "It hurts sometimes, y'know?"

Sawyer could see that hurt clear as day on her face. It was all he could do not to take her in his arms and soothe her, but he wasn't sure she'd want that. She took pride in being independent and strong. Then again, he wondered whether it was all pride or whether there wasn't a little defensiveness involved. Was she independent and strong because she wanted to be or because that was the only way she could manage on her own? And she was alone. He saw it now as he'd never seen it before. He wanted to soothe her for that, too, but he wasn't sure she'd want that, either.

Before he had a chance to do anything, she sighed. "So, anyway, Jack wasn't the most significant part of my life. He was just a physical presence while I went ahead and did what I would have done if I'd never married him. Sad, isn't it? It was a wasted relationship. I'm glad for his sake that he got out of it. He deserves more."

Sawyer wasn't so sure about that. In his book, Jack had had a gem in his hand and had dropped it. For his lack of care, he'd gotten what he deserved. "What about you? Don't you deserve more? I knew Jack. He was a nice guy, but he wasn't right for you. You were way ahead of him in most every way. He didn't satisfy you. He didn't challenge you. He didn't do anything for you that you couldn't do for yourself. So don't *you* deserve more?"

"I have my career."

"And what else?"

"Maybe that's enough."

"Is it?"

"More coffee, folks?" the waitress asked.

They swung their heads in her direction, startled by the interruption. Sawyer was the first to recover. "Uh, no. I'm fine. Faith?"

She shook her head.

"Just the check," Sawyer quietly told the waitress. When she tore it from the pad and put it on the table, he took it up in his hand. But he didn't look at it. His thoughts were elsewhere. "You sell yourself short, Faith. Maybe we both do. I say that Joanna is better off without me. You say that Jack is better off without you. Well, what about us? Don't we deserve excitement and happiness and fulfillment?" He opened his free hand to ward off an argument. "Yes, I know we get satisfaction from our work. But is it enough?"

Faith let the peripheral conversation, the occasional laugh or cough, the clatter of china on china fill in where she had no words. At last, she murmured, "I don't know."

He let out a breath. "It's ironic, when you think of it." Not that he had. He usually took life pretty much as it came, without deep thought to the future. "The satisfaction we get from our work was probably what did in our marriages. So now that our marriages are done in, is work enough?" He paused, held her sober-eyed gaze, shrugged. "I don't know the answer, either."

"That's a relief. It makes me feel a little less inadequate." She reached for the check.

"Don't you dare," he growled.

Carefully she retrieved her hand and tucked it in her lap. She heard the voice of command, and while there were times when she felt compelled to exert herself, this wasn't one of them. Paying for lunch at a diner wasn't going to bankrupt either one of them. Somehow it seemed foolish to argue over the bill.

Walking back to the car, he dropped an arm around her shoulder. It was a deliberately casual gesture. "You're a good girl, Faith."

She tipped her head up against his arm and gave him a pert smile, which seemed the least a good girl could do. It also told him that she wasn't grappling with heavy questions such as the one he'd posed. There was a time and a place for everything. Being away for the weekend with Sawyer had its own challenges without the pressure of intense philosophical thought. Time enough to brood about her future in the future.

They made several stops on the way back to the house—one to pick up a sleeping bag for Faith to match the one Sawyer already had, another to pick up a cooler and juice, milk and cheese for snacks, a third to pick up nails, scrapers and sandpaper. But rather than going right back to work, they took a walk. Sawyer wanted to show Faith the lay of the land, and she didn't argue. She loved the outdoors. Well beyond being a break from the city, walking through Sawyer's sun-speckled acres was a treat.

The land was beautiful. It rolled gently from one copse to the next, a world of greenery touched by the occasional crimson or gold. Though it was October, fall was reluctant in coming, as though it knew that a special something would be lost once the trees were bare. As those trees stood, a light breeze stirred their leaves. The same breeze lifted Faith's hair to her cheeks and dusted Sawyer's over his forehead. The continuity was satisfying.

The lakefront was broad and peaceful, perfect for skipping stones and imagining the delights of swimming on warmer days. There was even a dock, decaying to be sure but sturdy enough to hold Sawyer and, when she finally dared join him, Faith. For a long while they sat there, enjoying the silence of the afternoon. Neither of them thought to disturb it with words.

Faith was content. Sitting beside Sawyer on the broken-down dock, she felt she was privy to a moment out of time. She'd left her responsibilities behind in Boston. Her sole job was to...be. On impulse, she lay back on the dock with her hands as a pillow and closed her eyes to the sun. Its warmth was gentle, safe, lulling. Giving in to the soft smile that begged for release, she basked in the serenity of the day.

Looking down at her, Sawyer broke into a smile of his own. Her pleasure pleased him. He'd wanted her to like his place, and she did. She hadn't spoken as they walked, but he could tell from the look on her face that she was enjoying herself.

She might not have. He felt that he knew her well, still the focus of that knowledge was the career they shared. When it came to things beyond the law, his experience with her was more limited. For all he knew, she might have hated the house, hated the architect's plans, hated the rustic, uncultured look of the land. She might have hated the thought of sleeping in a sleeping bag on the floor in front of a fire, but when he'd pointed to a motel they'd passed, she'd given a firm shake of her head. Possibly she was out to make the point that she wasn't as soft as he thought, but if so, there wasn't a chance in hell that she'd win. Looking at her, all stretched out on the dock in her soft sweater and soft jeans, with her soft curves shaping both, he was more aware than ever of her femininity.

As was his body. The longer he looked at her, the faster his heart beat, and the faster his heart beat, the warmer his blood flowed. Somewhere in the middle of that, desire began to gather into a tight knot in his groin.

Moving to ease the knot before it grew painful, he pushed himself to his feet. The dock gave an ominous creak and an even more ominous wobble. He held his breath.

Faith raised her head to look up at him through the shade cast over her body by his. "Back to work?"

"Very carefully," he advised. He gave her a hand up, keeping the movement as smooth as possible, and waited until she'd left the dock before following her. By the time he was by her side, walking back through the tall grasses toward the house, he was in control once again.

His control lasted through the afternoon, but that was easy. He spent most of the time on the cone-shaped roof of the water tower, hammering away at the cedar shingles that had to be spaced just so, to prevent seepage of rain or snow. Yes, it was physical labor, but it demanded a certain amount of concentration from a roofer with his very limited experience. When he finally descended the ladder for the last time, it was with a sense of satisfaction in what he'd done...and a slight apprehension about the evening that lay before him.

For the first time, he wondered whether he'd been wise to invite Faith to stay overnight. Whenever he looked at her, even more when he came close, he felt the same quickening in his body. Sometimes it was in the area of the heart, sometimes in his hands, which itched to touch her, sometimes lower, where the ache was primal.

But he'd promised her that he would be the guardian of her virtue for the night, and he was determined to keep that promise.

Faith was counting on him for that, so she could relax and enjoy herself without having to exert a great deal of constraint. She worked some as Sawyer suggested, scraping and sanding chipped paint from the molding that framed the fireplace, the doors and the annex windows. But she was ready to take breaks at the slightest excuse, whether that was to convey a cold drink to the roof, to wander out in the meadow and chart the gradual descent of the sun or to sit on the grass and watch Sawyer at work.

She was impressed. He was surefooted and able as he carefully placed and hammered down each shingle. He'd long since tossed aside his flannel shirt, leaving him in the gray T-shirt that moved more easily with his shoulders and arms. As he built up a sweat, the shirt grew darker in patches. She was impressed by that, too, but in a different way.

Sitting on the grass with her arms around her knees, she wondered once again why she'd never noticed how virile he was. It seemed hard to believe that what she could drool over now had been before her many times before, and she hadn't appreciated it. Of course, she'd never before seen Sawyer in this kind of physical context, and besides, she couldn't have exactly drooled over him with Jack and Joanna in attendance. Still, she might have privately thought certain things, yet she hadn't. In that sense, she was impressed with herself.

When she married Jack, she had vowed to be faithful. She'd kept that vow. On occasion, she wondered if Jack had. She'd found nothing incriminating—not that she'd been looking—but there had certainly been nothing comparable to the note Laura Leindecker had discovered. Indeed, there had been times toward the end when Faith had almost wished Jack *would* have an affair, if only to make something happen. As it turned out, that hadn't been necessary. Emotional attrition finally took its toll.

So now, freed of the moral obligation of being true to Jack, she was seeing Sawyer in a different light. He turned her on. She was still appalled that they'd made love the way they had that Friday night, but she'd given up denying that the attraction was there. It existed, and it was strong. If she hadn't known it before this weekend, she couldn't miss it now. The question was where it would lead. Granted there was still the possibility that she was pregnant, but she didn't put much stock in that. She wasn't sure why— maybe gut instinct, or the romantic notion that when she conceived a child she'd know at the moment it happened—but she fully expected to get her period in another week. So that left the future very much open where she and Sawyer were concerned.

Where did she want it to go? She didn't know. And she didn't want to think about it. Thinking about it made her uneasy. She wasn't sure why, but it did. So she gathered herself up and went back to work inside until Sawyer called it a day.

"Hungry?" he asked as he leaned over the large sink on the wall of the annex that served as a kitchen. The bathroom sink was miniscule, something he was going to have to remedy.

Faith leaned against the most distant wall, watching him wash up. It was torture. He'd taken off the T-shirt and was sluicing water over his head and upper body with little concern for what splashed on the floor. Wet and gleaming, the sinewed twists at his arms and shoulders stood out well.

She took a shaky breath. "Uh-huh. I'm hungry."

"We could have dinner, then see a movie. There's usually something decent playing in Hyannis."

Faith wondered whether decent meant PG. She hoped so. She wasn't sure she could make it through an R-rated film without gnawing on Sawyer's neck. "That sounds good," she said, a little breathless.

Sawyer toweled himself off, reached for a clean T-shirt and pulled it on as quickly as he could. A sweater went over that, then he turned to her. "All set?"

With a nod, she led the way out through the tower, which was faintly lit now by the deep gold of the low-lying sun. Sensing there was a danger in lingering too long there, she hurried on.

Dinner was an enjoyable interlude before the movie, which turned out to have nothing to do with sex, for which Sawyer was eternally grateful. He didn't need the power of suggestion. His mind was providing plenty of that, and what his mind didn't respond to, his body did.

The air had cooled by the time they left the movie, and by the time they returned to the house, that cool air had seeped in through the uninsulated walls of the annex.

"Last chance," Sawyer warned. He was on the verge of lighting a fire, holding split logs in each hand. "I can still drive you to a motel."

Faith wore a jacket over her sweater, and though she could feel the night air through the layers, she wasn't about to seek a more cushy shelter. "Don't be silly. This is fine."

"It'll get colder before it gets warmer."

"So light the fire. If that's not enough, I'll crawl into my sleeping bag, and if that's not enough, I'll turn on your car and sleep there."

"You will not."

She laughed. "Just kidding. Go on. Light the fire." She was feeling high without having had a thing to drink. But that was Sawyer's problem. He'd agreed to see that nothing happened.

Sawyer set the logs on the grate, added a third and some kindling, then lit a match. The kindling took off instantly, the logs a few minutes later. Soon the flames were leaping high, sending off a welcome heat.

He sat back several feet from the flames and watched them in silence.

"A penny for your thoughts," Faith said softly as she scooted on her bottom across the floor until she sat at right angles to him. That way she could see both the fire and his face.

"I don't think you want to hear."

"Sure I do."

He remained quiet, though, debating the pros and cons of being honest. His decision came only after he'd dared a quick look at her. Lit by the fire, her features were warm and beckoning, making mockery of the promise he'd made. He desperately wanted to touch her, even if only in the innocent way he might have done two weeks, a month, a year ago. It occurred to him that his best hope of not touching her was to be perfectly honest about his needs.

"I'm thinking," he said in a voice that was low and a little gritty, "that I should be tired. I was up at six. I didn't get much sleep last night. I worked hard for a good part of the day. I had a huge dinner, and that movie was boring as hell. I should be ready to go to sleep. But I'm not."

"Maybe you're overtired."

"That's not the problem." Slowly and more deliberately this time, he shifted his gaze to hers. "I want you, Faith. I know I promised not to touch you, but I'm jumping around inside. Call it restlessness or whatever, but I want you."

She hadn't expected him to be so blunt. For a minute, she wondered whether he was simply trying to shock her. But he wasn't that kind of man. He didn't do things for effect unless he was in the courtroom, and he wasn't there now. The courtroom, the law, Boston were all far, far away. It was just the two of them sitting before a fire in his broken-down house on the Cape. Things were more raw here, unpadded, free of the city's gloss. That knowledge was what made the look in his eyes so stunning. It was a look of need that burned deep, and it wasn't for show.

Unable to handle the intensity of what she saw, she turned her eyes toward the fire. "I don't want that."

"I know. But I can't help it, Faith. I look at you, and it happens."

She could feel it happening to her, too. Their isolation, the fire, his physical nearness, the deep sound of his voice—those things would have done it alone, even if she hadn't seen the hunger in his eyes. "You said it wouldn't. I only came on that condition."

"And it won't. But you asked what I was thinking. So I told you."

He stopped talking, and for a time nothing broke the stillness but the crackle of the fire. Faith studied the flames, following them until they disappeared into the fireplace shaft, but if there was a pattern to their dance, she couldn't find it.

"Why is this happening, Sawyer?"

"This thing between us?" He snorted. "Because I'm a man and you're a woman."

"But we've been those things for a long time, now, and nothing happened before."

"It couldn't before."

"It could have. It's been over a year since Jack and I split and nearly as long for you and Joanna. We've seen each other several times since then, and nothing happened. Why now? Is it all because we had too much to drink last Friday night?"

"That may have started it," Sawyer conceded. He'd given the matter a lot of thought that week, mostly during the night when he'd lain awake while his body ached for what it couldn't have. "But the attraction—or the potential for it—must have been there a lot longer. We just didn't allow it to surface. That's all."

"Then you weren't aware of wanting me before that?"

"I didn't think about it. I didn't think of you in terms of sex. I thought you were pretty and sexy, but you were a friend. First you were married, and then when you were free, you were still a lawyer. A *lady* lawyer."

"Then my parents were right. I scare people away."

"That's not what I meant. I meant that you were a colleague of mine, and I took care to view you as one. Women have worked twice as hard to establish themselves as lawyers. Men have to work twice as hard to *see* them as lawyers instead of women." He considered her concern. "I can see where you might be intimidating to some men. You're attractive, vocal and successful. But so am I. So you don't threaten me in that way."

"Maybe it would be better if I did," she mused. Her tone was bittersweet, her expression sad.

Sawyer pulled himself up straighter. "Why do you say that?" When, after a hesitation, she simply shrugged, he reached over and turned her face to his. "Tell me why. What's so awful about our being involved with each other?"

"Nothing's so awful about it," she said, raising her chin to free it from his fingers. "I'm just not sure I want to be involved with anyone right now."

"You enjoy being alone? Are you a loner at heart? Was Jack's presence that much of a strain that you don't want anyone else in your life?"

"It wasn't a strain. It was just…disappointing."

"That's an enlightening comment."

She searched his eyes for mockery and saw none. "What do you mean?"

"The only way you could have found your marriage to Jack disappointing was if you'd had hopes for something better." His voice gentled. "We hope for what we want, Faith. What was it you wanted when you got married?"

She dropped her eyes. "I don't know."

"Sure you do. You just don't want to talk about it. Maybe you don't want to *think* about it, but maybe it's time you do."

"Why?" she asked, annoyed as she raised her head. Sawyer was putting her on the defensive, and she was prepared to fight.

He didn't blink. "Because if you're pregnant, you'll have to think about it. You'll have to think about lots of things you might not want to." He paused, watched the fight fade from her face, lifted his hand and stroked her cheek. "Have you thought about being pregnant?"

She swallowed. Still, her voice came out a shadow of itself. "I'm trying not to. I don't think I am."

"Would you want to be?"

"I don't know."

He ran his thumb along her jaw and spoke very quietly. "Yes or no. Would you want it?"

"I don't *know*," she insisted.

"Don't you want to be a mother?"

"Yes, but I'm not sure I want it *now*."

He dropped his hand to his lap. "Did you want it with Jack?"

"I used birth control when I was with Jack."

It was an evasive answer, but he let it ride. "Did Jack want it?"

"Sure." She took a breath, a lot easier now that he'd dropped his hand. She had trouble thinking when he touched her. "Babies went along with marriage, and he wanted it all. We used to argue a lot. I kept telling him the timing was wrong. It would have been hard for me to have a baby while I was in law school, and the law firm wasn't wild about the idea of maternity leaves, and then when I went out on my own, I had the full responsibility of a practice on my shoulders. I tried to explain to Jack that the timing was wrong then, too."

Sawyer wasn't buying into the bad timing theory. "You told me there were ways to do it. When we talked about it last week, you said that a woman can have a career and a baby."

"She can."

"But you didn't have a baby with Jack."

"I didn't *want* one with Jack!" Faith cried, then stopped short and hung her head. She took one deep breath, then another. The truth hurt, still it slipped from her tongue. "It wasn't the timing. It was him. If I'd had his baby, I'd have been locked to him, and early on I knew that wasn't right. By the time I graduated from law school, I think I knew Jack and I didn't have a future. And what my own instinct didn't tell me, my exposure to family law did. Kids don't make a marriage right. They don't make a bad marriage better. They may hold two people together who'd otherwise have split, but it's doubtful whether those people are happy, and if they're not, it's tough on the kids." She studied the fire in the hopes that it might soothe her guilt. "So that's it. I didn't want a baby with Jack."

"Would you want one with me?"

Her eyes shot to his. His features were golden and strong, but his look was cautious and, in that, vulnerable. She wanted to lie. She wanted to say that she didn't want a baby with anyone, but it wasn't true. For his openness, he deserved the truth.

"If I were to have a baby," she said in a near-whisper, "I'd want it with you."

A shudder ran through him. He sucked in an audible breath, closed his eyes for a minute, tried to get a rein on the flare of desire that accompanied the shudder.

Watching him, Faith was confused. "You want a baby?" she asked in that same near-whisper, then went on in a fuller voice. "If you wanted a baby, why didn't you have one with Joanna? She would have been a wonderful mother."

It wasn't the thought of a baby that made him shudder, as much as the thought of Faith having his. But he couldn't say that. It was too soon, even for him. He took several slow, deliberately calming breaths. "I could say that the timing wasn't right for us, either. Money was an issue. I didn't want a baby until I could afford to raise it with all the things I never had." But he'd never pictured a baby with Joanna's face the way he did now with Faith's. Nor had he ever before been shot through with desire at the thought of impregnating a woman.

He didn't say a word of that, yet his expression was telling. "Don't look at me that way," she begged. She felt it, too, the desire, and it made her uneasy. "Don't hope for it, please, Sawyer? You'll be disappointed."

But he didn't think that was possible. He didn't think Faith could disappoint him even if it turned out that there was no baby. She was incredibly bright and soft and vulnerable, and she wasn't half as sure of herself as she let the world believe. *He* knew she could be the best lawyer, the best wife, the best mother in the world. He also knew she could be the best lover, and though he'd made her a promise that he intended to keep, he wasn't averse to lobbying for his cause.

Coming up on his knees, he took her face in his hands, lowered his head and began his crusade.

8

"No, Sawyer—" Faith whispered, but the last of the sound was taken by his mouth. She flattened a palm on his chest. Within seconds, it was clutching a handful of his sweater, because seconds were all it took for her to feel as though the earth were being swept from under her. His mouth was hot velvet, stroking hers inside and out. His silken tongue found dark, hidden depths to plunder. His large hands held her head in a vise that was gentle but unyielding.

The first touch isn't much more than a token. It's kind of like a hello. The words echoed in Sawyer's mind, but they held no relevance. He and Faith had been exchanging tokens all day, looks and glances that were as expressive as any kiss. Same for hellos. He felt as though they'd been through hours of foreplay. Light tokens and gentle hellos were beyond him now.

That didn't mean he was rough. He could never be rough with Faith. She was too much of a woman for that, and besides, a good deal of his pleasure depended on hers. If she'd been quiescent beneath his hungry mouth, he'd have pulled back. But she was responding to his kiss, opening her mouth, offering her tongue, and while she wasn't aggressive about it, he didn't want that, either. Time enough for aggression once they were familiar lovers. For now, he liked taking the lead. It fed a very masculine need, and the fact that Faith didn't cut down that need as being macho or vain or archaic turned him on all the more.

If she was dynamite professionally because she knew when to stand firm, she was dynamite personally because she knew when to give. Even now, she was offering him the slender column of her neck, the graceful curve of her shoulders, the fullness of her breasts, which continued to surprise and please him. She was offering him her breath in short, wispy gasps, and the occasional tiny sound of excitement that slipped unselfconsciously from her throat.

She was offering him herself, and she'd warned him of that. She'd made him promise to be the one in control even when she wasn't. With a low groan, he dragged his mouth from hers. Slower to follow were his hands, which were splayed just under her breasts and didn't want to leave the warmth they'd found there. He forced them to. Sitting back on his heels, he brought them to his thighs and spread them there, and while the hardness of his limbs was nowhere near as appealing as Faith's warmth, they were something solid to hold.

"Disappoint me? Ahhh, Faith." His voice was hoarse, his broad chest working hard to still the thudding of his heart. "You couldn't disappoint me. Not in a million years. It keeps getting better. Incredibly. Better."

Faith was too stunned to say much for a minute. When she came to her senses, she was aware of wanting another kiss, of wanting much more than that. Need was snaking through her, coiling at certain spots, hurting. In a self-protective gesture, she wrapped her arms tightly around her middle, and though the tightness countered the hurt some, it did nothing for the chill of being out of Sawyer's arms. Groping for the sleeping bag that lay not far away, she pulled at its strings, artlessly unrolled it and dragged it around her shoulders.

It was a shield, protecting her from the intensity of his dark brown eyes. She still felt exposed, but that was her own doing and she sensed it was inevitable. Sawyer got to her. He touched her in places no man had ever touched before, and she let him do it.

"I think," she said in a slow, wavering breath, "that we need to put up a fence between us, something we can't see through."

Sawyer's lean mouth turned at the whimsy. "It wouldn't do any good. I'd know you were there, and I'd want you just the same."

Despite the intimacies they'd shared, the words were strange coming from him, Faith thought. Over the years he'd complimented her, said she was gorgeous and sexy and that he loved her, and she'd said similar words to him, but all in the good-natured way of friends. She couldn't get used to the idea that the joking was done, that the words and thoughts and feelings were for real.

"It's so strong," she whispered mostly to herself,

then raised her eyes to his. "Why is that? Is it because we've been without?" She caught herself. "I mean, I've been without. Maybe you haven't."

He twisted to reach for another log and one-handedly added it to the flames. As he watched it settle in and catch fire, he said, "It's not that. I've been with two women since Joanna, each for a night and neither one of them was particularly necessary or memorable."

"Why did you go with them? Was it just for the physical release?"

"Honestly?" He looked at her quickly, then looked back at the fire. It was easier to say something he wasn't proud of when he didn't have to risk seeing disappointment in her eyes. "I did it because I thought that was what I should be doing. I was a single man again. Right and left, friends were slapping me on the back, winking, making ribald jokes, speculating on how good I was probably getting it. It wasn't that I'd sleep with a woman because someone else expected me to, but after a little while, I guess the expectation became my own. I was beginning to think something was wrong with me because I wasn't panting after everything in skirts."

A self-deprecating smile tugged at the corners of his mouth. He drew up a knee and rested his forearm across it. "I used to do that. Way back, before Joanna, before Nam. I pretty much screwed my way through high school. I figured that I'd make up sexually for what I didn't have mentally. When it came to getting the girls, I was way ahead of the guys who drove around in their little red Corvettes.'' His smile vanished, his pose lost its indolence, and his voice dropped into a chasm of pain. "Then came the war. Once I took that hit, I wasn't thinking of sex. I was thinking of surviving. And when I realized that I would, I began thinking about life itself and the gift that it was. I began thinking that I owed it to someone upstairs to do something more than take a cheerleader under the stands during halftime.'' He took a deep breath. "Just about then I met Joanna at the VA hospital. Maybe because of where and why we met, sex was never one of our big priorities.''

Though he'd intimated as much before, Faith had trouble reconciling the potently masculine man before her with a relationship weak in sex. "Did you ever cheat on her?''

"No.''

"Did you ever want to?''

"No. Even after I was well, I had other things on my mind besides sex. I guess that's how it's been ever since. I have a comfortable life. My work is exciting. I convinced myself that if there was a right woman for me, she'd come along and I'd want her, and until that happened, I wasn't going to spend the goods just for the sake of the spending.'' He thought back to all he'd said. "So yes, I've been without, but no, that's not why it's so strong between us.''

Faith wanted to find a reason. She wanted to put a label on the need she felt so that it wouldn't be quite so frightening. "Maybe it's because of last Friday night. We'd been drinking. Our inhibitions were down. Maybe that set off the need for sex, and maybe it's the memory of that that's turning us on now.''

He doubted that. "If it was so, why would I get horny just thinking about what's under your sweater?''

"Because you remember Friday night. You remember feeling satisfaction. It's the memory that gets you horny.''

He shook his dark head slowly.

She tried again. "If it hadn't been for last Friday night, we'd still just be friends. We'd be laughing and joking the way we always have. We wouldn't be seeing each other in any kind of sexual way.''

"Maybe. Maybe not.''

"What is *that* supposed to mean?'' she asked, irritated that he wasn't grasping onto her suggestions.

His gaze was direct. He wasn't any more eager to see something negative in her eyes now than he'd been a little while ago, but he felt strongly that she should know how serious he was. "I think last Friday night was the catalyst for something that's very right.''

"You're saying that it was inevitable? Come on, Sawyer.''

That wasn't what he'd been saying at all, but the fact that she'd come up with it was telling. It made a statement as to the direction of her own thoughts, and she could deny them until she was blue in the face, but he wouldn't believe her.

"I think that if last Friday night hadn't happened, we might well have gone on forever and ever not knowing any better about what could be between us. But it did happen, and I think it happened *because* there's something between us. We could have stopped, Faith. We weren't that far gone that we couldn't have stopped if there'd been something so wrong with what we were doing. If we hadn't wanted it, we would have stopped. If the potential wasn't there, if we weren't attracted to each other, if we didn't *like* each other, we'd never have made love, no matter how much wine we'd had.''

She was listening. She didn't rush to argue with what he'd said. That gave him the courage to go a step further. ''It's not just sex. It's a lot more than that. We share a profession. We know each other, respect each other. We have fun together—we said that a whole lot on Friday night, and it's true. We've always had fun together. So now we desire each other, too, and that takes the relationship to a different level. It's the next step in the progression.'' He took a slightly shaky breath. ''I think we have the potential for a really deep thing here.''

Faith sat very still for several minutes. With a swallow, she tore her eyes from his and focused on the fire, but that didn't seem enough of a diversion. So she took the sleeping bag from around her shoulders, unzipped the top and shimmied inside. Moments later she was sitting cross-legged inside the thing, enveloped by it, looking at the fire again.

''Faith?''

''I'm a little cold.''

That wasn't what he wanted to know. "Talk to me, Faith."

But it was a minute before she did, and during that time she cursed herself as a fool for not running to the nearest motel, locking the door and burrowing in a large, lonesome bed. Then again, she wasn't a runner—at least she'd never been before—and she didn't like the way she was doing it now. She wondered if it was time she faced some of the things that had been hovering at the edges of her mind since Sawyer had made her his.

Her voice was small, muffled by the sleeping bag she hugged to her throat. "I don't want to be involved in a really deep thing."

He caught both her words and a thread of timidity so uncharacteristic that his insides clenched. Faith was a woman of strength. He couldn't fathom the cause of her timidity, didn't like it, resented it. "Why not?"

"I'm not ready for it."

"You're thirty-three."

"I'm not ready."

"Because of what you went through with Jack?"

She didn't answer.

"Faith?"

"I don't know."

"Talk to me. Tell me what you're feeling. Did your marriage to Jack leave a bad taste in your mouth?"

She thought for a minute. "Not really."

The pause worried him. He wondered whether

there was more to the story of her marriage than anyone knew. "Did he hurt you?"

"Hurt me? As in beat? Of course not."

Still her voice lacked its normal zing. She sounded distant, confused, as though something had indeed happened and she was just now trying to figure it out.

"What is it?" he coaxed, letting his voice tell her that he wanted to help. He was still a friend. No matter what else ever happened, he was still a friend.

Her eyes flicked from the fire to his, and the concern she found there tore at her. "Nothing. Really. My marriage was innocuous." But she paused, disturbed, and focused blindly on the floor. "It was disappointing. I've told you that. It was just a big fat zero."

"Better a zero than hell, I'd say."

She didn't smile. "I'm not sure. It's healthier sometimes to fight than to do nothing at all. At least that shows *some* kind of feeling. But there wasn't any between Jack and me. Not for a long time."

"And that bothered you."

"Yes, it bothered me. It wasn't the way marriage was supposed to be. It wasn't the way *I* wanted marriage to be."

"How was that?"

"Close. Warm. Fun. Satisfying. Supportive. I wanted my husband to be my best friend, but he wasn't. We were roommates. Period."

Sawyer was watching her closely, but he couldn't read anything more on her face than she was saying. "So you were wrong for each other. We all make mistakes. God only knows I did. And our clients? Mistakes all the time. So your marriage didn't work out. That's no reason to punish yourself by spending the rest of your life alone.''

"I'm not punishing myself."

"What would you call it?"

"Making sure I don't make the same mistake twice."

"That's crazy, Faith. I'm not like Jack."

Abundantly aware of that as she looked at him, she caught in a breath. "That's the problem."

He didn't make the connection. "What do you mean?"

"You're more vibrant than Jack. You're more fun, handsome, ambitious, interesting, sexy. You're more of just about everything. But I'm still the same."

He stared at her in confusion before muttering, "I still don't get it."

"You're *special*, Sawyer," she cried, then stopped when her throat grew tight. Dropping her eyes, she tried to regain her composure.

It was while she sat cocooned to her ears in the shiny blue sleeping bag with her eyes downcast that Sawyer began to understand.

"Babe?" When she didn't look up, he came forward, dug her chin from the slinky folds of the bag and tipped up her face. "You're afraid you can't make it in a deep relationship?"

She tried to look away, but he wouldn't allow it.

"Is that it, Faith?" He couldn't believe it. "Is *that* what you took away from your marriage to Jack?"

She swallowed the knot in her throat, but no sooner had she done that when her eyes filled with tears. Trying to maintain what little dignity she had left, she looked straight at him and said in a soft, wrenching voice, "I think the world of you, Sawyer. If I were to pick the one man I like and respect most, I'd pick you. I don't think I could bear it if we got into something deep and then it died."

What her tears started, her words finished. A tight fist closed around Sawyer's heart. "So you'd rather not try at all? Faith, that doesn't make sense!"

"It does to me. I'm the one who has to live with myself knowing that I've failed at something important."

"Is that what you've been doing for the past year? I thought you were fine after the divorce."

"I was. I was relieved to be free. But that didn't mean I didn't feel guilty about not making it work. Now, here *you* are, and suddenly the stakes are higher. You're more special than Jack any day."

Sawyer wasn't sure he believed that, but the fact that Faith did made the clenching around his heart ease into a gently kneading caress. Without another thought to what she might or might not want, he drew her, sleeping bag and all, to his chest. He pressed her cheek to his throat, where he could feel the velvet of her skin, while the long arm he coiled around her lower back anchored her to him.

"Y'know," he began softly, "for a bright lady, you can be damned dumb at times. Did it ever occur to you that I'd have an active role in whatever relationship we have? If I'm so special, would I really let it fail?''

She didn't answer. She was too comfortable being held in his arms, listening to the indulgent caress of his deep voice.

''Did it ever occur to you that you and I have a hell of a lot more going for us than you and Jack ever had? We're mature. We're established. We have money. We're both lawyers, and we're good friends. So now we're lovers. I think that sounds pretty nice.''

''It sounds scary,'' was her muffled reply.

''Not scary, because we're not making a life-or-death commitment. We're just going with the flow.''

''What flow?''

Closing his eyes, he tightened his arms around her and drew in a shuddering breath. ''The one through my veins that says I need you.''

''I don't want you to need me.''

''Too late. It's done.''

''Make it stop.''

''I can't. It's too strong.''

''But I want to go back to being just friends. It was more fun that way.''

''How do you know? You haven't given this way a fair chance.''

''I don't want to spoil what we have, Sawyer.''

''How about making it better? What would you say to taking what we have and building on it?''

She'd say that it was a dream and that she'd lost dreams in the past. She'd also say that it was a risk.

She could lose everything if it didn't work out. "I'm frightened."

Sawyer loosened his hold on her only enough to give him access to her mouth. He kissed her long and deep, offering her a taste of his hunger. It was his way of telling her not only how much he wanted her, but how satisfying she was. By the time he raised his head, her lips were moist and swollen.

He touched her cheek with a trembling finger. "Let's try," he whispered hoarsely. "Let's see how good it can be."

Faith wanted to do that so badly she hurt, still the fear remained. "What if it isn't?" she whispered back.

"Then we'll go back to being friends. We're both adults. We're experienced. We'll know if what we're doing isn't working." His gaze touched each of her features, pale in the fire's light and as fascinating to him as the spiraling tendrils of flame, themselves. "I'm not asking for a commitment. All I'm asking is that you give it a shot. Because I can't *not* do that, Faith. You've given me a taste, and now I want more." He paused and his voice went slack. "But maybe that's *my* problem. Maybe you don't feel the hunger."

"You know I do."

He let out a small breath. "So we share the problem. We could ignore it, but then we'll always be wanting and wondering. I don't want to live that way, Faith."

Looking up at him, Faith knew that they'd reached

a crossroads. She saw it in the virile planes of his face and the quiet demand in his eyes. He'd never make a scene. He wouldn't push her to do something she didn't want to do, but he knew her well. He knew that she wanted him. What he didn't know was whether she had the courage to take him.

It hit her then, suddenly and convincingly, that there was no contest. If she refused him, she'd be disappointing him anyway, and that was the last thing she wanted. She'd take the risk. She had to. Far better to see where the wanting would lead than to live forever with the wondering.

"I don't want to live that way, Faith," he repeated in a pleading whisper.

"I don't, either."

For what seemed an eternity, they looked at each other. Only gradually did they realize that they'd reached an agreement.

"So," she whispered, feeling strangely awkward. "What do we do now?"

"Sit and talk."

His answer pleased her, enough to allow for a glimmer of her usual spunk. "You don't want to just strip and do it?"

"No. I want to sit and talk."

She glanced down at her voluminous cocoon. "Like this?"

His lips twitched. "No. Not like that."

Setting her carefully on the floor, he added another log to the fire. When it caught flame, he turned to his own sleeping bag, unzipped it, opened it wide. Seconds later he had Faith's unzipped, and while she knelt by the fire, he connected the two. Then he sat back on his heels and looked at her. "I want to hear more about your family. Will you tell me?"

She eyed him curiously. "Why?"

"Because I'm interested."

"But I'm not them."

"You were once." He sent her a lopsided grin. "You've clearly evolved into a higher form of the species, but I've always liked history. It was the one subject in school that I paid attention to."

"History was more intriguing than girls?"

"Yeah. Less fickle. More predictable. Longer lasting."

"Does that mean you'll immerse yourself in my history and forget all about me?"

"Not a chance," he said too softly.

A frisson of excitement shot up and down her spine, making her shiver.

He misinterpreted the tiny movement. "You're cold." He tugged the double sleeping bag closer to the fire and held it open. Faith crawled in. He followed and took her easily into his arms. It was a minute before they'd settled comfortably, his body supine, hers angled into it.

She was cautious at first, but her caution didn't stand much of a chance against the feel of his body. It was long and solid, still it accepted her shape with surprising malleability. He was like that, she realized. Strong, yet flexible. That made the step they were taking a little less threatening to her. Gradually, she gave him more of her weight.

Sawyer did his best not to hug her hard in thanks for her trust. And trust was what it was about just then, he knew. She was trusting him to take care with not only her body, but her mind. She'd been hurt by her marriage, and though the hurt had been by default, the pain had been real. Now, curled next to him, she was vulnerable again. He rather liked that thought. He liked feeling responsible for her. The only problem was that he wanted to make love to her there and then, only he'd told her they'd talk.

Closing his eyes, he breathed in the sweet smell of her hair. Between that and the soft feel of her body, the weight of her hand on his chest, the bend of her knee over his, he was in an agony of bliss.

Faith felt something of what he did, but for different reasons. "This is so strange," she whispered.

"How so?"

"Being with you like this. We've known each other for so long. I keep thinking we're doing something we shouldn't be doing."

"We're not."

"You sound sure."

"I am."

She sighed. "Nice, to be so sure."

"You'd be sure, too, if you stopped thinking so much. *Feel* it, Faith. It *feels* right."

It felt more than right to Faith, but what he said was true. She thought too much. She wasn't used to relying on feelings. "I analyze things to death, I guess."

"Which is great for some things. It's one of the reasons you're such a dynamite lawyer. You look at a case from every possible angle before you decide on the best course of action, and you have to, because judges and juries don't decide things by intuition. They need arguments and facts. We don't."

But there were certain facts of which she was becoming increasingly aware, such as the fact that when he spoke his deep voice rippled through her, and the fact that his shoulder was just broad enough and full enough to make a wonderful pillow, and the fact that the scent of warm male after a day's work was surprisingly exciting.

Mostly she was aware of the fact that she wanted him. She might have joked about stripping and doing it, but there must have been a little wishful thinking in the joke. The more she relaxed against him, the more she tightened up inside.

Reflecting her thoughts, Sawyer shifted his lower body.

Faith tipped back her head and looked at him. The new log had brightened the fire, still his expression wasn't easily read. His eyes were dark, his lips firm, but it was only when the flames danced up with a sudden snap and a sizzle that she was able to see tiny lines of tension.

"Don't look at me that way," he whispered, not once taking his eyes from hers. "I'm trying."

"Trying what?"

"Not to take you right now. I said we'd talk."

"Why did you say that?"

"Because I want you to know that what's between us isn't only sex."

Faith knew that. "We've been good friends for a long time. You said it yourself—we had a lot going for us before we ever tried sex."

"Still there's a lot to say. Friends say certain things, lovers say others."

She kept looking at him. She wanted to say that she'd like to experience the lover part again before they got into deep discussions, but that seemed wrong. After all, she'd been the one putting him off.

"Help me, Faith," he growled. "I'm trying, but it's not easy."

But she couldn't look away. She was intrigued by his features, so carved and commanding, so taut with desire that she had trouble believing she was the cause.

He closed his hand over hers on his chest. "Why do you look so surprised?"

"I...uh..."

He began to move her hand in widening circles. "You don't believe that I want you?"

"I don't believe how much," she said guilelessly.

"Much. Very much." The circles edged lower as a wry grin pulled at his mouth. "And more by the minute." He had her hand at the snap of his jeans, but there the circles ended. After a minute's hesitation, he moved their hands southward to cover the raised ridge of hard flesh that pushed insistently against his fly.

Faith could barely breath. Vague glimpses of that other time, made hazy by the wine she'd had, brought the recollection of heat and length. But this was different. There was no haze, and the reality straining against her palm was far more than a glimpse. Heat, length, thickness, power—she was aware of all of those things as, with agonizing slowness, Sawyer inched her hand over him. When she saw his eyelids drift shut, even more when she heard the low, guttural moan that he couldn't suppress, she realized that the power was hers as well.

Shaping her fingers to better capture his strength in the stroking, she levered herself up and sought his mouth. He gave it to her, along with a wet, deep-seeking kiss that left her dizzy. It also left her far removed from thoughts of sensible discussions. What she was feeling, not only beneath her hand but deep inside her, was strong enough to decide the matter. She and Sawyer were making love then and there. Once they were done, they could talk.

She conveyed her decision to Sawyer by going in for a second kiss. This one was even more involving, and by its end, she was flat on her back with him looming above her.

"Last chance," he said. His low voice vibrated with need. His dark eyes were on fire from within. "Last chance, Faith."

Again she answered without a word, this time flattening both palms on his chest, running them up to his shoulders, then reversing direction and sliding them down over his chest and belly until they met at his burgeoning sex.

He moaned again, again helpless to hold it in, but he wasn't so helpless that he didn't know the import of the moment. Making love with Faith was going to be different this time than it had been before. This time they were stone sober. They knew what they were doing and why. And Sawyer knew that it had to be better than either of them remembered it being, if they were to have a shot at the future. He had to show her that when it came to sex, she was everything he'd ever wanted.

That was actually the easy part, because it was true. He couldn't control the hunger in his mouth when he kissed her, or his need to repeat the kiss from one angle, then another. He couldn't control the depths to which his tongue plunged in its search for hidden droplets of her sweetness. He couldn't control his need to nuzzle her neck, to inhale her scent as though it were life-giving oxygen, to nudge aside the crew neck of her sweater and nibble on her collarbone.

He told her of his pleasure in a myriad of wordless ways—in the smokiness in his eyes when he cupped her breasts, the tremor of his hands when he freed her from her sweater, the eagerness of his breath when he explored her through her bra. Whispered words came when he removed that wisp of lace and nuzzled her swollen flesh. He told her how beautiful she was, how responsive, and he showed her by chafing the pad of his thumb over her nipple until it was puckered and taut, then taking the hardened nub into his mouth and drawing it deeply between his teeth.

By this time she was holding tight to his shoulders, arching toward him, taking short, shallow breaths, and it was easy to go on. He undid her jeans and skinned them from her legs, then smoothed his hands over her panties until they followed. As though he'd been stifled before, when she was finally fully naked he couldn't touch her enough. With broad sweeps of his hands he covered her body from top to bottom. His palms were flatter over her throat, her hips, her legs; his fingers curved around her breasts and lower, on the focus of her womanly heat.

No, showing her how precious she was was the easy part. The hard part was restraining himself. At times he shook all over with the need for penetration. At times his breathing was heavy enough to wake the dead. But he was bound and determined to bring her to a fevered pitch of arousal before offering her the satisfaction they both sought.

She complicated things by moving against him in the most provocative, if innocent, ways. With slow turns and twists, silent yearnings spoke through her body, and then, when the turns and twists grew more frenzied and still didn't give her what she craved, she reached for his clothes. He thought he was safe as long as he was dressed, but she wasn't allowing that. One minute she was writhing in response to the sensuous glide of his fingers inside her, the next she was frantically struggling with his zipper.

"*Now*, Sawyer," she whispered. "Please. Now."

Grasping her wrists, he dragged them up and pinned them by her shoulders. His mouth closed over hers in a long, hot kiss, but if he thought that by breaking the momentum of touching he'd slow things down, it didn't work. The feel of her body beneath his was incendiary, adding the final spark to what was already glowing and ready to flame.

With a low moan, he left her long enough to tear his sweater and T-shirt over his head and work his pants down. Even before he tossed them aside, Faith's hands were on him.

Ironically that did slow him down. Her touch was too special to ignore, slender hands and curious fingers working their way through the hair on his chest, teasing his nipples, scoring his ribcage. He wanted to savor it, which was another way of telling her how good she made it for him, but when her hands slipped past his navel and found the grooves where his thighs connected with his torso, his resolve snapped. Coming over her, he drew her knees up to flank him and entered her with a single powerful thrust.

She gasped, stunned by the force of the filling, and for an instant Sawyer wondered if he'd hurt her. Her eyes were closed, her face shadowed. He couldn't make out her expression.

"Faith?"

But while he watched, she broke out into a slow smile, a crescent of sunlight in the midst of shadow, telling of the ecstasy she felt. "Don't stop now," came her whispered drawl. The sound was sexy to match the sultriness of her smile, both of which matched the feminine allure of her body, which was gold-tipped in the fire's dancing light.

Sawyer was driven just as much by what was going on in his head as what was happening to his body. He didn't believe that a woman could be as beautiful as Faith was and still be real. He'd set out to pleasure her as she'd never been pleasured before, but it seemed that in approaching his goal, the tables had turned. He'd never had a woman smile up at him like that, as though he were her world and she wanted no other.

He continued to bask in the heat of her smile until his body began to clamor for attention. Then he moved, slowly unsheathing himself, even more slowly and deeply returning to her heart. His breath pulsed against her lips, ragged between kisses. When soft sounds came from her throat, he increased the pressure of his mouth and stroking hands, and when she began to squirm against him, he increased the speed of his thrusts. He took pleasure in her every response, growing hotter and harder until the battle he fought against release seemed doomed. In a last-ditch effort to regain control, he paused, but in that instant, while he held himself as still as his quivering frame would allow, Faith arched into a powerful climax, and he utterly lost himself. Within seconds, bowing his back and pushing deeper than ever inside her, he vaulted into an orgasm of his own.

It was staggering, spasm after spasm of pent-up passion turned loose in her heated body, but Faith felt the powerful pulsations only as a counterpoint to her own shattering release. When the brightest of the star-bursts faded, she floated for a time in the limbo between heaven and earth. Only when Sawyer's breathing evened by her ear, when he slid his sweat-slick body to the side and pulled her over to face him did she open her eyes. What she saw in his nearly sent her aloft again. Neither the night or the dying light of the fire could hide the adoration there.

"How do you feel?" he asked in a whisper. He slid one still-shaky hand into her hair and stroked her scalp through the silken strands until he'd caught the last of his racing breath.

She searched for the words to best express it, but her mind was reeling again, this time from his look. "I feel," she finally managed to whisper back, "as though I've just finished off a magnum."

He grinned at her answer. "A little drunk?"

"A lot drunk."

"A little dizzy."

"A lot dizzy."

"But you didn't have a drop. Neither of us did, and still..."

She shaped a hand to his cheek, less sure with the trailing off of his words. "Still what?"

"Still...I felt like I was taken out of myself... immersed in you...lifted..." He stopped, feeling fool-ish and more than a little inadequate. "I'm not good with words."

But Faith had heard him in action more than once. "You're incredible with words."

"Not when it comes to something like this. I can

talk hard facts and make persuasive arguments, but I'm not a poet.''

"You're on your way."

But he shook his head. "I can't describe what it was like, Faith. It would take dozens of elaborate words and silvery phrases."

"Try plain ones."

"I love you."

She hadn't expected those particular words. Her eyes went wide, and for a minute she couldn't breathe, much less speak. Finally, diffusing the moment the only way she could, she tucked a hand against his neck and said softly, casually, "We've always loved each other."

"This is different, Faith. I love you."

"Like I love you."

"Only if you're talking forever." When she didn't have a comeback for that, Sawyer drew her to him. He cradled her head against his chest and the rest of her body fell into place, as though it knew from long experience just where to go. "Too much, too fast?"

After a minute, she murmured, "Mmm."

"Scary?"

"Yes."

"I'll give you time. I won't push. All I ask is that you let me see you." He endured a minute of gut-wrenching silence before prodding. "Will you let me do that?"

It wasn't so much that she'd let him, but that she didn't think she could keep him from it. Besides, it was what she wanted. She was still frightened; she knew she'd fear disappointing him even now, and it would be worse if she agreed to forever. Selfishly, though, she couldn't bar him from her life. She wanted more of him. She wasn't so inexperienced with men that she couldn't tell a good thing when she saw it.

"Faith?"

"Yes," she said, her breath stirring the drying hairs on his chest.

"We'll see each other?"

"Yes."

His body relaxed just that tiny bit, though not completely, because her nearness was stirring his senses. He ran a hand lightly from her shoulders to the small of her back, loving the satiny feel of her skin, which, even aside from his scars, was so different from his. He half-wished it were broad daylight so he could look at her. Strange, but he'd never seen her, really seen her naked.

That wasn't all that was strange. Curving a large hand over her bottom, he drew her closer. "Funny how things turn out sometimes."

His words registered through the light-headedness she was feeling again. "Hmm?"

"Before, when we started to make love, I wanted to show you how good it could be between us. I wanted to show you that it would be better than the first time, much better. I wanted to show you that you were all I've ever wanted." He paused, buried his face against her neck, breathed in the erotic scent of woman and sex that he found there, made a low sound in his throat. "I don't know how much of that I showed you, but I sure showed myself. You're it, Faith. You're what I want."

Being held so securely in his arms, feeling the strength of his body and its masculine warmth, Faith was just high enough to believe him.

9

That belief lasted through the weekend, and understandably so. Sawyer rarely left her side. He got her talking about all the things she didn't want to talk about and many of the things she did, and in both cases he interspersed the discussion with light touches and impulsive kisses. He wasn't fawning, though; his timing was perfect in that way. He knew when to touch, when to sit back and listen, when to ask a question, offer a comment, even tell her she was nuts. And he knew just when to take her in his arms and hold her tightly.

They made love often through Saturday night and then again on Sunday. Faith had never thought of herself as the multiorgasmic type, yet Sawyer brought her to peak after peak. His own stamina—and the multiple releases he, too, found—seemed further proof of his claim of love.

Inevitably, though, they had to return to the city. Faith put off thinking about it until the last possible moment. She felt she was living a dream and didn't want it to end.

Sawyer had no intention of letting that happen. Intent on showing her that things would be just as good between them in the city, he deliberately put off having dinner until they were back. He went with Faith to her place while she showered and changed clothes, then brought her to his while he did the same. Looking distinctly urbanized, they ate at Locke Ober's—again a deliberate move on Sawyer's part, since the restaurant, with its sense of tradition, was symbolic of the Boston they knew professionally.

Nor was he letting her slip away after that. He insisted on staying the night, and while she made token argument, sensing he was prolonging the inevitable, she let herself be convinced.

He didn't make love to her that night. "I've run out of condoms," he teased, and she almost believed him, given the number of times they'd made love. "I think I'll just hold you."

That was just what he did, and in so doing, he touched Faith more deeply than his sex ever had. Tenderly he cradled her against his large body until she'd fallen asleep, and though his hold shifted during the night with the turns both of them made in their sleep, at no point was she aware of being cold or alone.

At dawn's first light, he brought her awake with soft kisses and slow strokings, then proceeded to make love to her until she was crazy with need. No condom was necessary; he had other ways to protect her. When it was over, when she was lying utterly replete in his arms, he gave her a final hug before easing himself from the bed.

She watched him dress, feeling a loss with each part of his body that he covered. Before he left, he came to her. Planting both hands on either side of her pillow, he looked her in the eye.

"I know what you're thinking. You're thinking that we're both going back to work today and everything will be over. You're thinking that I'll sit in my office wondering what the hell the weekend was about. But you're wrong. I'll sit there thinking about you. I'll be wondering what you're doing for lunch and whether I can meet you, or whether I can manage to jimmy my schedule around so I'll bump into you in the courthouse. I'll be wondering what time you're getting home tonight and whether I can see you again." He took a breath. "I'll control myself during the day, Faith. I won't cut into your time. But I want you tonight." He stopped speaking on that declarative note.

Another time, Faith might have objected to his lack of a question—or if not objected to it, at least teased him about it. It was an extraordinarily chauvinistic thing to do, and she was a thoroughly modern woman. Just then, though, she wasn't feeling thoroughly modern. She was feeling reassured by his forcefulness, even turned on by it, though she sensed that the latter had something to do with the spark in his dark brown eyes, the random muss of his hair, the piratical shadow on his firm-drawn jaw. He was a quintessentially virile man, to which her body, still warm and tender from his loving, could attest.

Taking a slightly uneven breath, she said, "How about a study date?"

He got the message. "You have to work."

"I was planning to do lots this weekend, only a randy guy came by and swept me away."

He slanted her a grin. "Randy guy, huh? Yeah, I guess he did get carried away. But he'd do it again in a minute." He paused. "Study date? Is it that, or nothing?"

She nodded.

"Where?" he asked.

"My office. Around seven. We can bring in pizza."

Lowering his head, he fitted his face to the soft curve of her neck. He breathed in her love-warmed scent for a last minute before pulling away. "You've got yourself a date."

"He suggested we go on a date," Laura Leindecker told her on the phone later that morning. "Can you believe it? After being gone all weekend, he wants a date. After twenty-four years of missed dinners and canceled parties and late arrivals home, he wants a date."

Faith wasn't in the mood for adversity. She'd made a successful appearance in court on behalf of a client and was back in her office feeling cautiously optimistic about life in general and Sawyer in particular. She wasn't looking for anything that might upset the moment's balance.

Nor did she think that the idea of a date was so stupid. She'd made one with Sawyer. It was standard practice for a person feeling his or her way in a relationship.

"What did he suggest?" she asked pleasantly.

"Dinner at the L'Espalier. But that's not even my favorite restaurant. He *knows* what my favorite one is—or used to be—only he didn't dare suggest it."

"He was being considerate," Faith reasoned. "He knew how you'd feel. He was respecting your right to feel that way."

Laura wasn't fully convinced. "Maybe." Her voice grew wary. "He says he wants to talk."

"Then you should go. Listen to what he has to say. You'll be safe. He wouldn't dare act up in a restaurant."

"I suppose not." She sounded nervous. "But he's so good with words. He'll convince me of something. I know he will."

Faith tried to be supportive without yielding. "You're a strong woman, Laura. Don't underestimate yourself. You don't have to forget your grievances because he's taking you to dinner. But you do need to talk about what's happened and why."

"He'll tell me about *her*. He'll probably lie."

"Will he?" She let Laura think about that for a minute. "And if you don't want to talk about what's happened, talk about what you *want* to happen. Talk about the future. Talk about getting a divorce. Talk about the division of property. But talk. You have to communicate with each other."

"I don't want to communicate," Laura argued in a soft, pleading voice. "I want to file for a divorce. I want him to know that he can't do what he did to me and get away with it."

"You want to hurt him the way he hurt you, but will that give you what you want? Think about it, Laura. I can file a Complaint for Divorce with the court tomorrow, and a copy of the complaint will be served on your husband. Once that's done, it's a matter of public record, and once that happens, even though you can withdraw the complaint, something changes. Deeper feelings get stirred up. It's harder to go back. That's why you have to be really sure of what you want." She paused. "You're paying me to guide you through a divorce, but my first priority is your well-being. If your well-being is best served by a divorce, fine. If not..."

Her words trailed off, but she'd hit the right button, because Laura did agree to have dinner with her husband. Faith felt as though she'd achieved a minor victory. She would have called Sawyer to tell him if it hadn't seemed improper. It also seemed a little contrived. When push came to shove, she just wanted to hear Sawyer's voice.

It must have been her lucky day, because her wish was granted shortly after lunch when Sawyer stopped in at her office. Wearing a charcoal-gray suit with fine pinstripes running through it, he looked very professional and devastatingly handsome.

The first thing he did was close the door to her office. The second was to come around the desk and give her a kiss that shot professionalism to bits. The third was to drop into a chair and say, "Bruce Leindecker doesn't want the divorce at all. He says he loves his wife, and he says it on no uncertain terms."

Faith was a minute coming down from his kiss and another one focusing in on what he'd said. "He loves his wife."

"That's what he says," Sawyer declared in a satisfied way.

"Interesting," she mused. Her mouth still tingled. She was feeling pleasantly warm inside and decidedly close to Sawyer, which was probably one of the reasons why she tipped her hand. "Laura is still hurt and angry. But I think she loves him, too."

"Has she said that?"

"Lord, no. She says the divorce will teach him a lesson."

"She's being vindictive."

It sounded worse coming from Sawyer. "Not vindictive. She's just venting her anger."

"Maybe she's being too emotional."

"She has a right to be emotional."

"Too emotional? Nothing is accomplished then. Bruce is still trying to talk with her, but she won't listen."

"She will," Faith said with a satisfaction of her own. "He invited her out to dinner. I got her to agree to talk with him then."

Sawyer bobbed a brow in approval. "Good work, Faith. I knew you could do it. There's nothing like a woman to calm down another woman."

"Excuse me?"

"Women understand each other. They know what it's like to be highly emotional, so they can help each other when it happens."

"Uh…Sawyer…that is a gross overgeneralization. Not all women are emotional. Some never are. And your conclusion isn't even correct. The reason women understand each other is because they have a capacity for understanding and compassion that men just don't have. Laura Leindecker trusts me. That's why I was able to convince her to go to dinner with Bruce."

"And I think it's great. She has to listen to him for a change."

"Sawyer! She's been listening to him for twenty-four years!"

"Maybe she listens, but she sure doesn't hear."

Just as Sawyer was championing his client, so Faith championed hers. "She hears. And for twenty-four years, she's heeded. Laura has been a quiet, obedient, practically subservient wife. She has swallowed her complaints and made a comfortable life for herself. Suddenly she is betrayed. She doesn't trust Bruce the way she used to. Obedience comes harder now."

"Laura Leindecker is a highly emotional woman. She's making this whole thing far more complicated than it has to be."

"He *cheated* on her," Faith cried. "That's what started it all. How does it suddenly become Laura's fault?"

Sawyer sat forward, his eyes dark and intent. "I didn't say it was her fault. I said that she's complicating things. They might have patched up their differences without ever seeing a lawyer if she'd listened in the first place."

"Listened to what?"

"His explanations for why he had the affair."

"And why was that?"

"Because he was curious. A young, attractive woman came on to him. He's reached the age where he's flattered. He also knows dozens of men who've had affairs. He wanted to find out if it was so great."

"That's rubbish, Sawyer! Do you honestly believe him?"

"Yes, I believe him. I don't condone what he did, but I can understand how a man can be driven by curiosity that way."

Faith recalled what he'd told her about the months after his divorce from Joanna. "You weren't married then, Sawyer. You didn't hurt anyone by giving in to curiosity. Bruce did. He hurt Laura deeply. I'm not sure she can ever recover from that."

"Which is an emotional answer if I've ever heard one," he scoffed. "Of course, she'll recover. She'll listen to Bruce. He'll tell her that the affair didn't mean a thing, that he only saw the woman six times and—"

"Six times! If it didn't mean a thing, why did he see her six times? Did it take him six times to satisfy his curiosity, or was it six times before his wife found out? Did he think she *wouldn't* find out? If the affair was so meaningless, why in the *hell* did he leave that note in his coat?" She raised flashing eyes to follow Sawyer, who'd risen and was coming toward her. "Bruce Leindecker was wrong, Sawyer. He betrayed a woman who'd done nothing to deserve it. If he thinks she's going to easily forgive and forget, he's crazy. And so are you if you agree with him.''

Curving his hands around the arms of her chair, Sawyer bent at the waist, ducked his head and put his cheek by hers. In a deep voice that gave individual emphasis to each word, he said, ''I do not agree with what he did. I think he was wrong in having that affair, and I'd think it even if his wife *had* deserved it. I believe in fidelity, Faith. I always have.''

His message took the wind from her sails. Or maybe it was the deep rumble of his voice. Or the warmth of his cheek. Or his clean male scent. Or the looming presence of his body. But the fight went out of her as quickly as it had come. She grabbed his necktie just below its knot and held on.

When he spoke again, she heard a suspicious smile in his voice, ''I do love it when you get emotional.'' He kissed the tip of her ear. ''It's a definite strength. A man likes it when a woman shows some fire. It means she cares.'' He dragged his mouth across her cheek.

''I care about all my clients,'' she argued, but weakly.

''You care about me. That's what this is about.''

''It is?''

''Um-hmm.'' He nibbled on her jaw. ''You want to know that my judgment is sound. You want to be comfortable with the sides I take. You want to be sure that we're playing the game. You don't mind my representing the bad guy as long as I don't buy his cause, particularly in this case. Am I right?''

He was, but she didn't want to say so lest she dislodge his mouth from her lower lip.

"So," he breathed softly, "that's another way I need you in my life. You're my conscience. Without you, my chauvinism is apt to run away with itself."

Having had just about enough of his teasing, Faith tugged him down by the tie for a full-fledged kiss. When it was done, she lingered for a minute with her eyes closed and her lips a breath from his. She could stay that way forever, she knew, but if she did that, Sawyer would be onto her in more ways than one. And she had work to do.

Pushing him away the same way she'd pulled him in, she said, "Go. I have a brief to write."

He headed for the door. "Are we on for seven?"

"We're on."

They didn't bring in pizza after all, but imported corned beef sandwiches from the sub-basement deli in their building. By ten, Faith was nearly falling asleep at her desk.

"I can't imagine why," she quipped, yawning. "You've bored me so that I've done nothing but sleep for the past two nights."

Sawyer laughed and said nothing in his own defense, principally because he intended to keep her awake for part of a third night as well. And she didn't fight him. When they went back to her place and he took her in his arms, she went willingly. She moaned her delight when his mouth refamiliarized itself with her body's nooks and crannies, and when her hunger took a different twist, she even became the aggressor. It was a new role for her. Passion drove her on, but during the brief instances when the newness of it stunned her, Sawyer had ready words of praise and love.

Once she fell asleep that night, Faith was completely out of it. She didn't stir when Sawyer kissed her at dawn, didn't waken when he climbed out of bed and dressed, didn't open an eye when he softly called her name.

He left her a note. It was the first thing she found after she realized she was alone, and it helped in easing her disappointment at finding him gone.

Sweetheart,
You were sleeping so soundly that nothing short of a buffalo stampede would wake you. Not having any buffalos on hand, I tried some kissing and touching, but even that didn't work. So I'm off. I have a committee meeting at six tonight that will probably drag on until nine. I'll call you then.

Love, Sawyer.

Faith lay back down and held the note to her breast for another few minutes while she slowly woke up. Then she climbed from bed and got ready for work. Just before she left, she folded the note and tucked it into a pocket of her briefcase.

That was a tactical error.

Each time she opened or closed the briefcase,

which was often on a day filled with appointments outside the office, she stared at the pocket and thought of the note. By late afternoon, she'd taken it out and read it numerous times, had traced the letters of his name with her finger, had even held the folded paper to her cheek as something he'd touched. It was the last time, when she folded the note and tucked it away not in her briefcase but in her bra, that she began to realize the extent of her feelings for Sawyer.

They overwhelmed her. She didn't like that at all, because she felt she was losing control. It wasn't like her to put love letters in her bra, any more than it was like her to wait for the phone to ring, or be disappointed when she woke up alone in bed, or plan her days to free up her nights.

In an appallingly short time, she'd grown dependent on seeing Sawyer. But she'd never been dependent on a man like that before, and she didn't think it was healthy.

That was why, when Sawyer dialed her number at nine-thirty that night, the phone went unanswered. Thinking she might have run out to do a quick errand, he tried again in fifteen minutes, then in fifteen after that. So he ruled out a quick errand. On the vague chance that she was still working, he tried the office number, but the answering service ruled out her presence there.

He decided that she had to be out with friends, and while one part of him thought that was just fine, the other was furious that she hadn't bothered to tell him. A simple phone call would have done it. If he'd been out of the office, she could have left a message. That would have been the considerate thing to do, since she knew he'd be calling.

By eleven, when there was still no answer, he began to worry. So he tossed on a jacket and jogged along the waterfront until he reached Union Wharf. He rang her bell. When that produced no response, he rang it again. And again.

After the fourth or fifth stab, Faith opened the door. The relief he felt was instant, then instantly forgotten in the face of the decidedly disgruntled expression she wore. "What do you think you're doing, Sawyer?" she asked. Though her voice was imperious, her appearance was anything but. She wore a white nightgown that went from her throat to her wrists and toes, and a long white terry wrap robe over that. Her face was clear of makeup. Her hair was brushed back behind her ears.

Sawyer thought she looked tired and more than a little vulnerable. That softened his annoyance, but only a bit. "I was worried," he barked. "I've been trying to reach you for two hours. Why aren't you answering your phone?"

"I was out. I just got back."

"Where did you go?" he demanded.

"I was visiting a friend. Not that it matters. Sawyer, I don't have to report to you."

"You knew I'd be calling. I left you a note this morning and told you that. If you weren't going to be here, you could have let me know. Then I wouldn't have worried."

Her fingers whitened on the doorknob. "You shouldn't have worried anyway. I'm a big girl. I've been taking care of myself for a while now. You should have just assumed that I had other plans, instead of assuming I'd be home waiting for your call."

Sawyer put both hands on his hips and glared at her. "I never assumed you'd be waiting. I assumed you'd be around. I assumed that since it was a work night and you complained about getting no sleep, you'd be tired."

"I am," she declared. "So thank you for coming over, but you can go home now. I'm going to sleep."

She made to close the door, but a well-placed foot stopped its progress, and he slipped inside. "Not without me, you're not." He shut the door behind him.

The determination on his face was so strong that she took a step back. "What do you think you're doing? You can't just barge in here like this!" She lowered her voice to a more controlled tone. "I want you to go home. I want to be alone."

"You don't want that," he said.

"I certainly do."

He shook his head and reached for her, catching her in his arms and holding her there while she protested.

"Let me go, Sawyer."

"Not until you tell me what's bugging you. Was it the note? Was it that I didn't call you during the day? Or stop down to see you? Was it my having to work tonight?"

"No!" She pushed against his chest, but it was an unyielding wall of muscle. "I don't care whether you work or not!"

"Then it was one of the other things."

Still she squirmed. "*No!* You don't have to call me during the day, or stop down to see me. In case you hadn't noticed, I have work to do, too. I have as demanding a career as yours. I don't have time to dally between cases any more than you do. Let me *go*, Sawyer."

Ignoring her cries, he held her tightly. "I'd make the time to dally with you if I thought you wanted it," he said in a quieter voice that flowed gently by her hair, "but I've been trying to respect your career. I know how hard you work. I know how much your work means to you. And I know how good you are at it. So I'm trying not to get in the way during the day. That was why I left the note. I figured it would carry over to tonight. I need to see you at night, Faith, and if I can't see you, I need to know why. Why didn't you call if you weren't going to be here?" He took a shuddering breath. "I love you, Faith. I know you don't want to hear those words, so I've done my best not to say them, but I do love you. Did you think I wouldn't worry when no one answered the phone after so long?"

The fight had left her with the quieting of his voice, and by the time he was done talking, its gentle, almost pleading tone had done a job on her anger. Closing her eyes, she let herself lean against him. "Oh, Sawyer."

"What?" he asked hoarsely. "What does that mean?"

"It means I don't know."

"Don't know what?"

"What I was thinking. Feeling. Doing."

He stroked her back with large, knowing hands. "Sure you know. You're just not ready to verbalize it. You're tired. You're in a lousy mood. Maybe it's that time of the month."

Tired or not, she probably would have hauled back and socked him if she hadn't heard the teasing in his voice. "That, Sawyer Bell, is the most bigoted thing you've said yet. Men have moods just like women. I have every *right* to be in a lousy mood. I'm not tired. I'm *over*tired."

Without another word, he moved her under one arm and headed for the bedroom. When she'd taken her robe off and was tucked into bed, he sat by her side. "You're right. You need sleep."

She studied his handsome face. "Are you leaving?"

"You want me to."

"You said you were staying."

"But you'd rather sleep alone."

She darted a glance at the empty side of the bed. "There's room here. I'd hate to send you out in the cold."

"It's not very cold. I can jog back the same way I came."

"Or you can jog back in the morning." She paused, then before she could ask herself what she was doing and why, whispered, "Stay, Sawyer. I want to sleep with you."

Sawyer stayed.

"The woman won't talk," Bruce Leindecker complained to Sawyer when he called on Wednesday morning. "I took her to dinner, and we sat like two very civilized people. She listened to what I said, but she wouldn't talk."

"She just sat there, mute?" Sawyer asked.

"Not mute, exactly. She offered simple answers to simple questions, but when I asked her to tell me what she felt, she just stared at me. Let me tell you, that stare hurt."

"Did you tell her that?"

"No."

Sawyer rubbed the back of his neck. He was getting a little tired of hand-holding, though he was being paid well to do it. "Maybe you should have."

"Then she'd have done it more. She wants to get back at me. She wants to hurt me like I hurt her. It doesn't seem to matter how much I apologize. She's still angry. Maybe she really does want out."

"Maybe she needs more time."

"Maybe I should just give in and file for divorce myself. If I did that, she'd talk. She'd say she doesn't want the divorce after all and attack me for wanting to dump her." He paused. "Reverse psychology. It's not such a bad idea."

Reverse psychology had worked for Sawyer the night before. As soon as he'd said he was leaving,

Faith had changed her mind about wanting him to. He suspected Laura might do the same—and it had nothing to do with a sexist bias, because he used the tactic repeatedly with difficult male clients. No, he suspected Laura might do the same because he was privy to information Faith had passed on. If Laura did love Bruce, she'd protest the divorce as soon as it became a serious consideration.

But gut instinct told him the timing wasn't right for that. "Wait. Just a little longer. Reverse psychology can work, or it can backfire. It would be a tactical error to threaten something and have her call your bluff. Backing down would weaken your position." He debated the alternate courses of action. "You're still living at home, aren't you?"

"Yes."

"Okay. So keep talking to her and keep after her to talk back. Don't be discouraged. She's been badly hurt, and it's the kind of hurt that won't go away with an apology or two."

"But I'm legitimately sorry. She knows that. She knows me."

Sawyer reflected on the things Faith had said. "She may have thought she did once, but she never imagined you'd go off and have an affair. So in addition to being hurt, she's probably afraid to trust you, or her own instincts where you're concerned. You have a long road ahead, Bruce. This isn't something that a woman can easily forgive and forget." He rocked back in his chair wearing a small, smug smile, thinking that Faith would be proud of him. He might be a chauvinist, but he wasn't beyond being broadened.

Bruce wasn't as pleased as he was. "From the way you talk I'd do just as well to toss in the towel now. Are you saying that I've got to *grovel*?" Sawyer could almost hear him straightening in his seat and donning his executive front. "I won't do that, Sawyer. I may love the woman, but *no* woman—or man, for that matter—runs me into the ground like that. I'm not without pride. If she pushes me too far, I'll give her a divorce with pleasure."

"I doubt it will come to that. Just give her time."

Bruce agreed to do that, and Sawyer hung up the phone. His first thought was to call Faith, but he meant what he'd said about disturbing her. It wasn't as if something momentous had happened with the case. And besides, they had a date for lunch.

That gave him the excuse he needed. Lifting the phone, he dialed her number. When she came on, he said, "Was that twelve-thirty or one? What did we finally decide?" Their plans had been a little muddled in Sawyer's dash to throw on his clothes and get out the door in time to jog home, shave, shower, dress and make an eight o'clock breakfast meeting.

"One," she said softly.

"Ahhh. Okay. That's great." He paused. "Everything going all right?"

"Fine. Busy." But she didn't hang up.

"Great. Hey, listen, I'm sorry to bother you, but I just wasn't sure and I didn't want one of us waiting."

"You're no bother."

"Maybe I should have run downstairs, just poked my head in and asked you in person."

"*That* would have bothered me."

"Why that?"

"Because you're a distraction any way you come, but seeing you in the flesh is the worst."

"Is that a compliment or a complaint?"

"You figure it out," she said with a smile in her voice. "You can tell me what you decide at lunch. Goodbye, Sawyer."

Having lunch with Sawyer was a different experience because for the first time, eating at a local restaurant that they both frequented separately, they were seen together. The place was packed with acquaintances and colleagues, most of whom probably assumed they were discussing matters of law.

Faith knew the truth, though. This wasn't a legal lunch but a social one. She enjoyed being with Sawyer. She also enjoyed being *seen* with him, and that bothered her a little. Professionally, she had her own identity. She wasn't out to get respect riding on another lawyer's coattails. She earned her own respect.

No, the pride she felt didn't have to do with her image as a lawyer. It had to do with her image as a woman, and that was what bothered her. She felt more feminine when she was with Sawyer. She felt that people would *see* her as being more feminine, and it surprised her that she cared. But she did care, which meant that she had much more to lose if the relationship ended.

More and more, it seemed, she was growing dependent on Sawyer. He was in her mind whenever her mind wasn't occupied with work. She was quickly coming to expect that she would see him for dinner and then spend the night with him. She feared she'd be crushed if he decided he needed a night alone.

She thought of being the first to do it, of telling Sawyer herself that she couldn't see him that night and sticking to it this time. If she was the one who rejected him, it wouldn't hurt so much, she figured. The problem with the figuring was that she really wanted to see him. Making excuses would be a bit like biting off her nose to spite her face.

On and off through Wednesday afternoon, she wallowed in a state of indecision. Then Laura Leindecker called.

"My husband won't leave me alone," she cried. "We have to do something. I'm not sure how much more of this I can take."

Faith was beginning to feel like Dear Abby, and she didn't think she cared for the role. "What's he doing?"

"He is waging a campaign to win me over. First it was dinner, then breakfast. He's calling me from the office three or four times a day wanting to know how I am and what I'm doing. This is very strange for a man who absented himself from my life for so many years."

"He loves you."

"He's scared."

"Scared of losing you."

"Scared of losing the house or the Mercedes or the millions he'll have to settle on me."

"From what I understand, he's got more than enough to go around."

"But he's making me crazy with his constant attention. It's gotten so that I feel guilty going *shopping* because he can't reach me in the stores."

Taking a breath in a bid for patience, Faith said, "Maybe if you gave him a little encouragement, he wouldn't feel that he has to work so hard to convince you of his devotion."

"I don't want his devotion!"

"I thought you did. I thought that was what this was all about. You were complaining that he was never around."

"He wasn't," Laura cried, "but I got used to that. I structured my life so that I had things to do, and I have even more things to do now that the children are grown. But they're women's things, like luncheons and bridge club and garden club, and Bruce is going to be in the way."

Faith sighed. Much as she tried to respect Laura's dilemma, she was tiring of the game. "What is it you want?"

"I want things to be the way they were! I want Bruce to go his way and me go my way, and when he's not on a business trip or tied up late at the office, we can see each other. Maybe I do want him to be devoted, but I don't want to be smothered."

"And you really don't want a divorce."

"No, I don't want a divorce."

"Do you love him?"

"I've loved him for so long that I wouldn't know how *not* to love him."

"Have you told him that?"

"How can I? It's the only lever I have left."

The phone line was silent for a minute. Then, slowly and quietly, Faith said, "Please, Laura, please talk to him. Tell him what you've just told me. He doesn't want a divorce any more than you do. There's nothing wrong with your marriage that some good heart-to-hearts won't fix. Tell him how you feel. Not just the surface things, but deep down inside."

"That won't work," Laura said sadly. "We've never been able to talk that way with each other."

"Maybe it's time you started."

"But I can't trust him. I did once, and look where it got me."

"He made a mistake. He knows that and regrets it." Faith sighed. "Either you give him another chance, or we file papers tomorrow. You have to decide one way or the other, Laura. It isn't fair to you, it isn't fair to Bruce, and it isn't fair to Sawyer and me. We're lawyers. It's our job to push for reconciliation, but we can't lead you through that the way we'd be able to lead you through court. We're not trained to be marriage counselors. You have to decide which you want."

Laura made a small, bewildered sound. "Why do *I* have to make the decision?"

"Because," Faith said with sudden insight, "you're the one with the power."

10

Through the rest of the day, Faith thought a lot about women and power. They underestimated themselves, she decided. Too often they bought society's line and associated men with the power, and maybe that was true in the business sphere, but not necessarily in the personal, more emotional one. Laura Leindecker was in an enviable position. She knew what she wanted, could reach out and take it if she decided to, and in that sense she held her husband in the palm of her hand.

Sawyer wasn't one to be held in any woman's palm, and Faith wouldn't have it any other way. Still, there were times when she wished he wasn't so sure of himself and his feelings. Then she wouldn't feel so weak by comparison.

Such was her line of thinking that night at his place, which was where he took her after work, and while she watched him grill steaks and toss a salad, she felt increasingly powerless. Her relationship with him seemed to be barreling forward, and as it went, she had less and less control over it.

There were three possible reasons for that, she decided. The first was that Sawyer was right, that the relationship had lain dormant for years and now, under newly favorable circumstances, was ripe for the growing. In that case, the relationship itself, the male-female dynamics were controlling Sawyer and her.

The second possibility was that Sawyer was the one in control, that he was the force behind the onrush of their relationship. He was more aggressive than she was. He was the one making sure that they spent every free minute together, and it was at his insistence that they were sleeping together every night.

She didn't fight him very hard, which raised the third possibility. She wondered if it was simply her own *lack* of control where Sawyer was concerned that was letting things snowball. Because they were snowballing. The more she was with Sawyer, the more she enjoyed being with him, and the more she had visions—fleeting, granted, but nonetheless vivid—of being with him forever.

She might have felt a semblance of power if Sawyer was running around trying to please her. But he wasn't. He knew what he wanted, which just happened to be what she wanted. He was perfectly at ease, perfectly comfortable, perfectly happy doing things that were satisfying for them both.

He was also attuned to the tiny crease that showed up between her eyes from time to time, and whenever he saw it, he immediately and deliberately filled her mind with different thoughts. Still, the issue of who she was as a woman, whether she was an active or a passive one, whether she had any real power, shadowed her. Long after they returned to her condo, after they'd made sweet, sexy love, she lay awake thinking about it. Each time she came near to an understanding, Sawyer would do something in his sleep—tug her closer, kiss her, whisper her name—and the issues became muddied again.

She knew one thing. He did love her.

She knew another thing. She did love him.

What she didn't know was whether she was the type of woman who could sustain a relationship like that, and whether she could bear it if she wasn't.

Thursday morning came too soon. She'd found no answers to her questions and she'd had far too little sleep. It was an easy matter to keep her eyes closed while Sawyer dressed, but it was harder to ignore him when, as was becoming his habit, he came to sit beside her before he left.

"Plans for today?" he asked, smiling at her sleepy look.

"I don't know," she mumbled flatly.

"Uh-oh. You're tired."

"Mmph."

"And cranky. Should I let you get into the office and call you there?"

"Mmm."

Without another word, he bent his head and placed a chaste kiss at the corner of her mouth, then left.

Because he'd read her so well, she was in an even worse mood, and because she was in an even worse mood, she felt even weaker, which made her more angry. She stomped out of bed, went into the bathroom and slammed the door.

Then she found that she'd gotten her period.

"Good morning," came Sawyer's deep voice on the phone shortly after she'd arrived at the office.

"Hi, Sawyer," she said in a no-nonsense, businesslike way.

He got the hint. "You're busy."

"Very."

"Can I see you later?"

"Uh, I don't know." She flipped through her desk calendar—unnecessarily since the day's appointments faced her on a single page. "I have one meeting after another."

"Lunch?"

"With the mayor."

"I'm impressed."

"Don't be. It's business."

"Then I'm jealous."

"No need. It's me and six other women."

"Sounds kinky."

She sighed.

"Okay," he conceded. "I'll call you later."

He tried her at two o'clock, but she hadn't returned from lunch. He tried her again at three, but she'd returned and left again. When he tried her at five, she was with a client. So he left a message for her to call him when she was free.

She called him at six-thirty, and her tone was anything but encouraging. "Sorry I've missed you. It's been one of those days."

"You sound tired."

"I am. I think I'll go home and go to bed."

There was no mistaking the lack of an invitation. But then, Sawyer had had a premonition all day. "Is something bothering you?"

"I just said it. I'm tired."

"Beside that."

"What could be wrong?"

You could be uptight about us. You could be feeling crowded. You could be missing your freedom. "I don't know. You tell me."

"I'm tired, Sawyer."

"But if I said that I'd go home with you and work while you sleep, you'd say no, wouldn't you?"

It was only a minute before she said, "Yes."

"You want to be alone. Why?"

"Because I want to sleep."

"You wouldn't sleep better if I was there?"

She heard his gentle teasing, but she was determined to resist its lure. "That's an egotistical question if ever there was one."

"I sleep better with you than I do alone."

"Sure. Sex is a powerful sleeping pill."

He abandoned gentle teasing. "Even when we don't make love, I sleep better when you're with me. What's wrong, Faith? What's eating you?"

"I'm tired."

"Talk to me. Tell me what it is."

"I'm tired."

"Tired of me?"

"Tired, period. I need sleep. Alone."

He listened to what she was saying and tried to read between the lines, and though he could imagine what the problem was, if she wouldn't talk, they couldn't work it out. He debated pushing her, but the idea that she might be legitimately tired kept him from it. He figured he could give her a little time.

"Okay," he said. "You go on home and get your sleep. I'll call you in the morning."

"I'll be in court in the morning."

"Then I'll call you before court."

"No. I'll be with my client before court."

"Then I'll call you after court."

"I don't know when I'll be back."

"I'll keep trying," he said, less indulgently now. "You're being crabby, Faith, and I don't think it has anything to do with being tired. It has to do with us, but unless you tell me what it is, I can't do anything about it." He was pushing her, just as he'd told himself he wouldn't do moments before, but he was helpless to stop. "There may be times when you'd like to turn back the clock and make things between us the way that they used to be, but you can't do that. I can't do it. I don't *want* to do it. So we'll talk. If not now, later." He meant every word he was saying, and then some. "You're running, Faith. But I run faster. I'll always catch up. Remember that."

He hung up the phone before Faith could tell him how dumb what he'd said was. And it was just as well. The more she thought about it, the more she realized that it hadn't been such a dumb thing to say at all. Sawyer had an advantage over her that had nothing to do with physical size or strength. It had to do with determination. He knew what he wanted, and he wasn't letting it get away.

She was flattered. More than that, she was gratified. More than that, she was touched and touched deeply—so much so that at times during Thursday night, she felt herself on the verge of tears. She was frightened. She wanted Sawyer, but didn't want to want him, and she was terrified of losing him. She was alternately confused and frustrated and angry.

By Friday morning, she was feeling totally washed out. At some point during the night, her mind had pulled a temporary blank and allowed her to sleep, but it hadn't been enough. The light of day illuminated all the things she preferred to have left hidden in the dark.

Grateful to have something to fully occupy her mind, she met with her client at eight, then went to court. By eleven-thirty she was back at her desk, and though she hadn't come up with an answer to the Sawyer dilemma, she found herself willing the phone to ring. He said he'd call. When he didn't, she felt angry—not so much at him, but at herself for being disappointed.

Being disappointed was her lot in life, she decided in a fit of self-pity as she threw papers and files into her briefcase and headed for the law library to work. If she wasn't in the office, she reasoned, she wouldn't be there to hear the phone not ring, which was some improvement on the disillusionment of waiting and wishing.

Sawyer found her at the library. It was nearly four, and neither the dimming light of day nor the heavily shaded lamp on the table could hide his irritation. Slipping into the wooden armchair beside her, one of eight at the long mahogany table, he leaned close and whispered, "Where in the hell have you been? I've been looking all over for you."

"I've been here," she whispered back. She didn't know whether to be pleased that he'd found her or not. Her heart didn't wait for her to decide; it was beating faster than it had moments before.

"Why wouldn't Loni tell me?"

"Because she didn't know. I said I was going out. I didn't want to be disturbed."

Sheltered by knitted brows, Sawyer's eyes skipped toward the two other men at the table. Though they seemed engrossed in their own work, he carefully kept his whisper low. "Well, you're going to be disturbed. We have to talk, and we have to talk now."

"I'm working now."

But he was already closing the books she'd been using. "We'll go to Timothy's. It's right around the corner. We can take a quiet booth at the back."

"Timothy's is a bar."

"So a drink might do you good."

"I don't drink."

"It might loosen up your tongue."

"I don't need a drink to loosen my tongue. I don't want to talk."

"Come on, Faith. You're pulling a Laura Leindecker, and what was it you told her? That she had to share her feelings with Bruce?''

"They're married. We're not.''

"Through no fault of mine. I'd have asked you last weekend and seen the deed over and done by now if it had been up to me.''

"Well, it's not.'' Her whisper took on a panicky edge. "Sawyer, what are you doing?''

He was gathering her papers together and stuffing them none too neatly into her briefcase. "We're getting out of here.''

"I'm not leaving.''

"If you don't,'' he said, pausing in his work to lean extra close, "I'll give you a slow...wet...deep... kiss.''

Faith could hardly breathe. Sawyer's nearness was bad enough, but when his breath fanned her ear and his words heated her insides, her resolve was more fragile than ever. Still she clung to it.

Grabbing her papers from Sawyer's hands, she put them into the briefcase herself. "You'll give me no such thing. I'm going back to the office.'' Snapping her briefcase shut, she stood.

He was right beside her when she left the table. Before she could go far, he closed a hand around her arm. "You're coming with me.''

"No way.'' Her voice remained a forced whisper. "It's over, Sawyer. I've made up my mind. I apologize for having led you along, but this relationship isn't for me. It's too time-consuming. Too distracting. Too demanding. I can't possibly be what you want, and I'm exhausted trying.'' With the carpeted room left behind, her heels beat a rapid tattoo on the floor.

"It's the fighting that's exhausting you," Sawyer declared. Though they no longer had to whisper, he kept his voice low. That didn't blunt its urgency. "Give in. Let it happen. Say you love me."

They trotted down the broad marble stairs, nodding to a judge coming up, but not pausing. When they burst through the large double doors and hit the street, Faith tried to turn in the direction of her office. Sawyer firmly propelled her the opposite way.

"Sawyer, I can't," she cried. "I have work to do."

"Work will wait. This won't."

"What's the big rush?"

He strode on holding her arm, his dark eyes straight ahead. "Yesterday was unbearable. Last night was even worse. I won't let things go on like this. I spent years watching my marriage fizzle, and I didn't fight because I didn't care, but I care about this. You say it's over. I don't believe that. If you want to convince me, you'll have to do it now."

"I just did," she argued. "This relationship is too much for me to handle."

"Bullshit."

"Say what you want, but it's true."

"You were handling it just fine at the start of the week," he argued, generating anger to cover up the unsettled feeling in the pit of his stomach. "Nothing's changed since then, except that you started getting *scared* that you couldn't handle it. So you decided not to try. That is *cowardly*, Faith, *cowardly*!"

"So I'm a coward. That's as good a reason as any why it won't work."

They reached Timothy's. Sawyer kept his hand in firm possession of her arm while he drew her through the door. "Two of whatever's on tap," he called to the bartender as he swept down the long bar to a booth near the back. It was the only free one. The bar was filling up with happy-hour patrons. The noise of their chatter didn't bother him, any more than the dimness of the place did. Both provided a certain privacy.

When he'd successfully nudged Faith into the booth, he slid in opposite her. Without preamble, he pierced her with vibrant brown eyes and picked up where they'd left off. "What you're doing is totally out of character. You weren't meant to be a coward, Faith. Professionally, you're one of the bravest women I know. You've taken on cases that other lawyers have refused, and you've won. You've taken on Boston's staid legal community and done more for family law than any other lawyer in years. And you haven't done so badly personally, either. You stuck with Jack because you believed in marriage, and when it became obvious that it wouldn't work, you had the courage to let go."

She sputtered out a laugh. "That's a contrived way of looking at it. I *failed* in my marriage. I stuck with it because I *didn't* have the courage to let go. I only got out when it became obvious that there was nothing left. It didn't take courage at that point."

Sawyer wanted to scream in frustration. He didn't

understand why she had to be so hard on herself. "Why do you insist on seeing the worst? Why do you choose the most pessimistic view of what happened? There were positive things in your marriage. I saw them." He gave a small, impatient shake of his head. "But I don't want to talk about your marriage to Jack. That's over and done. I want to talk about us."

Resting her head against the wood back of the booth, Faith eyed him forlornly. "Nothing's changed. Back when we were at the Cape, I told you my worries. They're the same."

"You're afraid you'll disappoint me."

"And myself."

"Monday, Tuesday and Wednesday—were you disappointed?"

She thought back to the warmth in which he'd kept her cocooned, and she couldn't lie. "No. I wasn't disappointed then."

"Because you enjoyed what we did. You enjoyed being together."

She nodded. "But I grew dependent on that, and I don't like being dependent."

"So you tried to put me off. That's why you wouldn't see me yesterday or last night."

She tried to defend herself. "Things between us have gotten too intense too fast. We need to cool off."

"But we won't. Out of sight doesn't mean out of mind." He spared only a moment's glance at the frothy steins the bartender brought. "I thought about you all last night. Can you honestly say you didn't think about me?"

"No. I thought about you."

"And you decided that since you like me so much, you shouldn't see me so much. You don't want to become too dependent on me—or have me become too dependent on you. You don't want to be disappointed if something goes wrong." Arms on the table flanking his untouched beer, he leaned forward. "That is *convoluted logic*. It's like saying that a lamp makes reading a breeze, but you'll sit in the dark so you won't come to rely on the lamp in case the bulb blows. Well, hell, if the bulb blows, you get another. Things can be repaired. So can relationships, if they mean enough to you."

Eyes holding hers, he sat back. "The Leindeckers are together again. I got a call from Bruce after lunch telling me that they've kissed and made up."

That was news to Faith. "Really?" she asked cautiously.

He nodded.

"I haven't heard anything about it from Laura."

"Because you've been incommunicado since lunchtime. She called. Loni told me."

In the brief respite from her own troubles, Faith allowed a small smile. "They're forgetting about the divorce?"

"They're going to try to work things out. Bruce was extremely grateful to us. Especially to you. Laura told him that you kept pushing for a reconciliation. You kept telling her to talk with him and tell him how she felt." He paused, wondering if she was getting the point, deducing from the unenlightened look on her face that she wasn't, deciding to make it himself. "How can you preach that and not do it yourself?"

Her eyes widened. "I *am* talking to you. You know how I feel."

"You wouldn't talk with me yesterday, and, no, I don't really know how you feel. You've never said whether you love me or not."

"I have, too. I've told you I love you dozens of time."

"As a friend."

She swallowed. Closing her eyes for a minute, she thought of those warm, wonderful times when she lay in his arms. "And as a lover," she said, sending him an unknowingly adoring look. "I could never respond to you the way I do, or do the things I do to you if I didn't love you."

For the first time since he'd found her at the library, Sawyer experienced a faint lightening in the area of his heart. Again, he leaned forward, this time beseechingly. "Then give it a try, Faith. Don't fight it. Don't ruin the present by worrying about the future." When he saw the skepticism on her face, he hurried on. "Listen, I don't know what the future holds. None of us do. Life doesn't come with a road map telling exactly what turn to take when in order to get to a prescribed destination." That thought gave him pause. "Where do you want to go? Do you know? Supposing you were to look ahead ten or twenty years, what do you see yourself doing, being?''

"I see myself as a successful lawyer.''

"What else?''

"I don't now.''

"What do you mean, you don't know? What do you *dream*?''

"I don't know.''

"You do, but you won't say. You *are* as bad as Laura Leindecker.''

"And you're like Bruce. You won't leave me alone. Why not, Sawyer? That's all I'm asking, just to be left alone. Is it so difficult to do?''

Straightening his shoulders, Sawyer took a different tack. Keeping his voice low, he said, "Okay. I could leave you alone. I could let you go back to the kind of life where work is basically all there is. I could let you bury yourself in the law. I could disappear from your life. Does that sound better?''

It sounded devastating, but she didn't say it.

He went on. "We could do what we did for years, bump into each other at conferences or seminars or political fundraisers. Maybe we'll even have another chance to work with each other. We could meet by accident on the street once in a while, date other people, sleep with other—''

"I don't want that.''

"What?''

"To sleep with other people. I don't want it.''

"You don't want to do it yourself, or you don't want *me* to do it?''

Her eyes blazed. "Both. Either."

"But you don't want to sleep with me."

She didn't answer.

Her lack of response stirred Sawyer's frustration, which in turn made his voice sound harsh. "What do you want, Faith? Beyond a career, what do you want? There must be other things. You're a woman capable of warmth and love. Don't you want an outlet for those?"

She stared at him. Oh, she knew the answer to that one, but she was afraid, so afraid to give it, and Sawyer knew that.

"Why is it so *hard*?" he asked. "You always used to talk to me. You used to tell me everything. Why can't you now?"

"Because things have changed between us!"

"We're more involved."

"Yes."

"So we should be sharing even more." He reached his limit. If she wouldn't say it, he would. "Damn it, Faith, I want it all! I want you as my law partner, my wife and the mother of my kids, and I think that if you can be honest with yourself and with me, you'd admit that you want those things, too."

Hearing him put it all into words was nearly more than she could bear. "I do," she cried softly, "but it's a dream. That's all. A dream. Life has ways of taking unwanted twists. I've seen it happen time and again. We hope for things, and when they don't happen, disillusionment sets in. I'd be devastated if that happened with us."

"It won't. We love each other. We have so much going for each other."

"But I'm a lawyer," she said, and tears began to gather on her lower lids. "I'm a lousy cook and a lousy cleaner, and I wouldn't know how to change a diaper if my life depended on it."

"So you'll learn. We'll learn."

"But I'm not even pregnant!" she cried and, feeling an awesome ache, she scrambled out of the booth and ran toward the front of the bar.

Swearing, Sawyer tossed several bills on the table to pay for the beer they hadn't touched, and took off after her. He caught up half a block from the bar. Snagging her by the wrist, he hustled her into the nearest doorway, out of the line of rush-hour foot traffic. His hands went flat against the granite on either side of her shoulders. His large body prevented her escape.

"When did you get it?" he demanded, furious enough to momentarily overlook the tears streaking down her cheeks. "Your period. When did you get it?"

"Yesterday morning."

"And that's when the trouble started." It suddenly made sense. "You figured I'd be disappointed that you weren't pregnant."

"*I* was disappointed," she cried. "That was bad enough."

"Because you wanted to have my baby," he said. The gentleness that hit him then, the heart-wrenching care dissolved whatever anger he'd felt. His hands left the granite, slipped around her back and drew her snugly against him. "Ahhh, Faith. I do love you. You have to be one of the most bullheaded women I've ever met in my life, but I do love you."

"I wanted to be pregnant."

He recalled the way she'd talked when they'd first discussed the possibility, and knew she was telling the truth. "Why didn't you tell me? I wouldn't have had to bother with—"

"I couldn't tell you. I didn't know how you felt."

"You could have asked."

"But then I'd have *known* how you felt."

"Mmm, that makes sense."

"It does. If you hadn't wanted a baby, and it turned out I was pregnant, you'd have been disappointed. Same thing if you'd wanted a baby, and I *wasn't* pregnant. So I was better not knowing."

He tucked his head lower against hers. "You're never better not knowing, Faith. And you're never better keeping things to yourself. A relationship is about sharing. You know that. You've counseled any number of clients on it, most recently Laura Leindecker. So if you can tell them to communicate, why can't you do it yourself?"

"Because I'm emotionally involved, and when I'm emotionally involved I can't think straight!"

"You've got that right, at least. As far as the rest goes, you're out in left field."

"See? I'm a disappointment already."

"Did I say that?"

"You were thinking it."

"No, ma'am. I was thinking that I love it when you're out in left field, because it gives me a chance to play hero. It feeds the macho in me."

She groaned, but the sound was barely muffled by his coat when he pulled back, took her hand and started off. She had to trot to keep up. "Where are we going?"

"Somewhere."

"Obviously. Sawyer, I can't go anywhere," she cried as the breeze dashed the tears from her cheeks. "I have work to do."

He didn't miss a step as they turned onto Beacon Street. His hand kept hers well in its grip. "Y'know, I'll bet you didn't give Jack half this much trouble when you agreed to marry him."

"I didn't give him any trouble, and I haven't agreed to marry *you*."

"I'll bet you just smiled and said yes, when there were dozens and dozens of reasons why the marriage wouldn't work."

"I was young and stupid. So was Jack. We wanted marriage more than we wanted each other."

"And the irony of it is," Sawyer went on as though she hadn't spoken, "that here we are with dozens and dozens of reasons why a marriage between us *will* work, and you're driving both of us crazy dreaming up problems."

"I'm not dreaming them up!"

"Some people do that, y'know. They can't bear the thought of happiness so they throw stumbling blocks in their own way." Pulling Faith faster to cross Tremont Street before the light turned, he yelled, "Taxi!" The cab that had just dropped off a customer and was starting to pull away from the curb stopped. Too involved in defending herself to question him, Faith slid in at Sawyer's urging and resumed the discussion the minute he joined her.

"I *do* want to be happy. I've never deliberately thrown stumbling blocks in the way of that."

"No?" To the waiting cabbie, he said, "Copley Place."

"Copley Place?" Faith echoed. "Sawyer, I have to work." But the cab was already on its way, as were her thoughts. "I'm being cautious, that's all, and there's nothing wrong with it. I've already flunked out of one relationship. Every day I see the tattered remains of other relationships. I'm thinking of *you*, Sawyer."

"Okay," he said in a lower voice, "think of me." With the creak of aged vinyl, he shifted on the seat to face her. "Think of how much I want you, not only today and tomorrow but for all the tomorrows after that. Think of how much I want to work with you and travel with you and finish the place at the Cape with you and have kids with you—" When she looked stricken by the last, he hurried on. "Not right away. I'm glad you're not pregnant. I want you to myself for a while. Besides, if you were pregnant, you'd think that was why I wanted to get married, when it's not."

"I haven't agreed to *any*—"

The rest of her protest was lost in the kiss Sawyer

gave her. It was a sweet kiss, powerful in that sweetness. It said he loved her, loved her even when she was being difficult. That was very much what he was thinking, and when—after trying the kiss from several different angles simply because her lips were so pliant—he finally lifted his mouth from hers, he felt the theme worth discussion.

"You can't disappoint me, Faith," he said. His face was inches from hers. Almost reverently he held her chin in the notch of his hand. "You can't *possibly* disappoint me. You're one of the best lawyers around. Whether you win or lose a case, you give it your all, which is more than most do and as much as any client can ask. As a wife, you'll be smashing, and I don't give a damn whether you're a lousy cook—"

"I'm lousy at it because I hate doing it," she blurted out. She was having trouble thinking with the taste of him lingering on her lips and his face so close and his voice so gentle, but she had to speak up. She feared it might be her last chance. He was so near and dear. Her resolve was slipping. "What kind of wife hates to cook?"

"The kind who has a full-time job outside the home and doesn't have the time or energy to spend working over a stove. And there's nothing wrong with that. I don't expect you to be superwoman. If we need a cook, we'll hire one. Same thing for when babies come. I may be traditional about some things, but I'll never ask you to stop working unless that's what you want. Besides, you said it yourself—babies and careers are mixing better and better these days."

"I don't know anything about mothering."

"Neither do I. So we'll learn. There are books all over the place, and classes." He brushed the tip of his finger by the corner of her eye as he visually devoured her features, then went on in a voice that was even lower and slightly rough, "And as a lover, you're more than any man could imagine. No woman has ever turned me on like you do. No woman has ever done to me what you do." He took in a short, sharp breath. "The other night...what you did... where your mouth was and your hands..."

He didn't have to finish. Faith remembered the moment well. She'd shocked herself, not only with what she'd done but with the pleasure she'd taken in the doing. A soft, sexy smile stole over her lips. "Liked that, did ya?"

"Yeah," he whispered. "I liked it."

"I've never tried it before. So, it worked?"

"Oh, yeah." Even in memory it was working, but the jolting of the cab through the traffic was a reminder of where he was. "You're dynamite, Faith."

She liked the sound of that. "But what happens when I get older? Will I still be dynamite when my hair is gray and my breasts sag and I have cellulite on my thighs?"

"By that time, I'll be bald and paunchy and my eyesight may be so lousy that I won't be able to see the cellulite on your thighs."

"You'll never be bald and paunchy."

"How about my eyesight? Will you love me even if I can't see straight?"

"Of course I will. What kind of dumb question is that?"

"The same kind *you're* asking," he said and gave her a minute to realize it before saying, "There are two points here, m'dear. The first is that you're dynamite to me because of who you are, not what you look like. The second," and he sobered, "is that none of us knows what the future holds. We have to look at what we have now and decide whether we think it's strong enough and positive enough to make us happy today and optimistic about tomorrow." He lowered his voice again, this time in urgent coaxing. "Come on, babe. You know we can make it. Stop fighting. Give it a chance."

But before she could respond one way or the other, the cab pulled up at the Marriott Hotel. Without so much as a look at the meter, Sawyer stuffed a ten-dollar bill into the cabbie's outstretched hand, opened the door and pulled Faith out. Keeping her close by his side, he entered the hotel at a broad stride.

"What are we doing here, Sawyer?"

"You'll see."

They were passing through the lobby, and for a minute Faith thought he was going to take a room on the forty-fifth floor and make wild, passionate love to her overlooking Boston. It was a romantic idea, and it wasn't beyond him at all, she knew. When they passed the registration desk without stopping, she wondered if he'd taken a room in advance. "That was a presumptuous thing to do," she murmured, half-flattered, half-annoyed.

"What was?"

"Booking a room without even knowing whether I'd come. You assumed I'd cave in, didn't you? Beth Leindecker said her mother always did that. Bruce snapped his fingers, and she came running."

"I should only be so lucky," Sawyer said under his breath, then added, bemused, "I didn't book a room." Sure enough, they passed the bank of elevators and headed toward the escalator that led to the mall level.

"Oh." She frowned. "Then what are we doing here?"

"Going shopping. Watch your step. Hold on. That's it."

"Sawyer, I've been on an escalator before. But why are we going shopping? And why here? Prices are exorbitant here. I have to warn you, I'm almost as lousy a shopper as I am a cook."

"I don't believe that. You always look spectacular."

"Sure, because I'm drawn to the most expensive item on the rack. It happens every time, like there's some kind of radar flowing between the price tag and my head without my seeing a thing."

"That's fine. Price is no object. I want the best." Fingers laced through hers, he drew her off the escalator, toward the first store on the left.

"The best what?"

"Diamond ring."

Her eyes widened as they passed through Tiffany's vaulted portals. She tugged back on her hand and whispered loudly, "What are we *doing* here, Sawyer?"

Her tug didn't faze him. He strode right along. "Buying you an engagement ring. I want all the bozos in Boston to know that you're taken."

"But we're not engaged."

"We certainly are." He produced a dashing smile for the woman behind the counter. "We'd like to look at engagement rings—something substantial, maybe with a few little stones on the side—sapphires, rubies, whatever goes with diamonds—you know what I'm talking about."

The saleswoman certainly did. She had carefully removed several spectacular possibilities from the showcase and placed them on a bed of navy velvet before Faith could find her tongue.

"Sawyer," she murmured out of the side of her mouth, unable to take her eyes from the rings, "uh, Sawyer, I think we should talk."

Leaning close, he said in the same side-mouth murmur, "Definitely. What do you think? I think the blue stones look a little cold next to the diamond. I like the green, the emeralds. They go with your eyes."

"My eyes are hazel."

He looked into them. "They look green to me. Maybe it's what you're wearing." He dropped a quick glance at the long pleated skirt, sweater and blazer she wore, a blend of solids and plaids in plum and moss. "Super outfit," he mouthed. His eyes glowed in appreciation.

Cheeks growing pink, Faith tore her gaze from his

and forced it back to the rings. "I can't accept one of these."

"Why not?" He put his mouth by her ear and whispered, "I love you. I'll always love you. I'll love you until the sun sets in the east, until the rivers run dry, until Santa gets stuck in a chimney in Winnemucca, Nevada—"

"They're too elaborate." She looked beseechingly at the saleswoman. "Haven't you got something a little simpler?"

Sawyer started to argue, but before he could do much more than tell her she deserved the best, the saleswoman produced two rings that stilled his tongue. Both held single stones, one round, one pear-shaped.

"Ahhh," Faith breathed in awe. Smiling, she carefully lifted the pear-shaped ring from the velvet. "This is more like it."

"Don't you want something a little more showy?"

"You're the one who wants something showy. It's the old macho pride." She continued to hold the ring, spellbound by its sparkle. "This is special. Simple but exquisite."

He had to agree that it was, still he'd envisioned something different. "Maybe we should look at something with more than one diamond." He turned to the saleswoman. "How about it? Something with one big stone and two little ones on the sides? Maybe with diamonds all the way around?"

Faith was still admiring the pear-shaped diamond when the saleswoman added two other rings to those already out. Faith didn't like either as much as the one she still held in her hand. "They're too busy. If a stone is beautiful, it should stand on its own." She took a soft breath. "I like the solitaire."

"You're worried that the others are too expensive, but I'm telling you, Faith, money isn't an object here. If I can't splurge on the woman I love, who *can* I splurge on?"

"Sir?" the saleswoman spoke up a bit nervously. "About the ring your fiancée is holding—it's the finest quality diamond we carry." She cleared her throat. "Given that and its shape and size, I'm afraid it's the most expensive one I've shown you."

Quickly but carefully, Faith set the ring down. "I should have known," she muttered. "I do it every time."

But Sawyer was lifting it, taking her left hand, slipping the ring on her third finger. It fit perfectly. "Simple and exquisite." He grinned. "We'll take it."

"We can't take it," Faith whispered, but the sharpness she'd wanted to put into the whisper fell prey to the beauty of the ring on her finger—that, and the contrast of Sawyer's long, lean hand holding hers. "We...I...can't."

"You can," he said softly, and something in his tone brought her eyes to his. They were dark and intent, filled with love and a kind of bare-hearted expectancy that made Faith tremble. "You can," he whispered. "You can do it, Faith. You have the power to reach out and try, and that's all I'll ever ask of you. Reach out and try. Give it your best shot.

Nothing's a given in life, but there's so much hope in this. I want it. You want it. Together we'll make it work.'' Her eyes went wider, as though he'd said a magic word, but her lips remained pressed close together. ''What do you say? Wanna give it a try?''

She wanted that more than anything, and in that moment she realized the extraordinary power she did have. She had the power to bring Sawyer happiness— and the power to find it herself. Yes, there was a risk. The stakes were frightfully high. But the alternative? Standing there, looking up into Sawyer's face as she could quite contentedly do for years and years, she knew that the alternative was no alternative at all.

Words eluded her, but words weren't needed. Her answer came in a short nod, a soft smile, the tears that filled her eyes and the arms that went around his neck. When he slid his own arms around her and crushed her to him, she felt a joy she'd never known. She also felt a confidence she'd never expected.

He was right. Together they'd make it work.

Take 3 of "The Best of the Best™" Novels FREE
Plus get a FREE surprise gift!

Special Limited-time Offer

Mail to The Best of the Best™

3010 Walden Avenue
P.O. Box 1867
Buffalo, N.Y. 14240-1867

YES! Please send me 3 free novels and my free surprise gift. Then send me 3 of "The Best of the Best™" novels each month. I'll receive the best books by the world's hottest romance authors. Bill me at the low price of $3.99 each plus 25¢ delivery per book and applicable sales tax, if any.* That's the complete price and a savings of over 20% off the cover prices—quite a bargain! I understand that accepting the books and gift places me under no obligation ever to buy any books. I can always return a shipment and cancel at any time. Even if I never buy another book, the 3 free books and the surprise gift are mine to keep forever.

183 BPA A4V9

Name	(PLEASE PRINT)	
Address	Apt. No.	
City	State	Zip

This offer is limited to one order per household and not valid to current subscribers. *Terms and prices are subject to change without notice. Sales tax applicable in N.Y. All orders subject to approval.

U808-197   ©1996 MIRA BOOKS

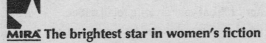

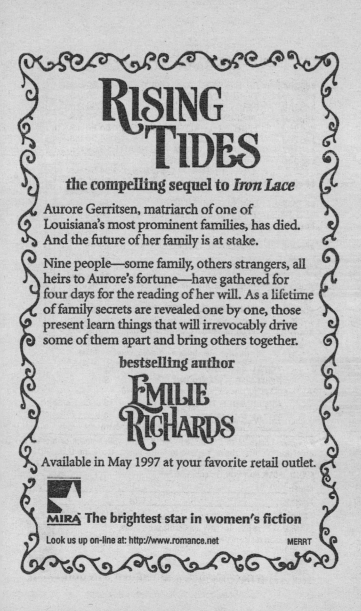